W9-BEV-183

Have
to Have It

Also by Melody Mayer

The Nannies

Friends with Benefits

Have to Have It

by Melody Mayer

Delacorte Press

a nannies novel

Published by Delacorte Press
an imprint of Random House Children's Books
a division of Random House, Inc.
New York

This is a work of fiction. Names, characters, places, and incidents
either are the product of the author's imagination or are used fictitiously.
Any resemblance to actual persons, living or dead, events, or locales
is entirely coincidental.

Text copyright © 2006 by Cherie Bennett and Jeff Gottesfeld
Front cover photograph copyright © 2006 by Getty Images

All rights reserved.

DELACORTE PRESS and colophon are registered trademarks
of Random House, Inc.

www.randomhouse.com/teens
Educators and librarians, for a variety of teaching tools,
visit us at www.randomhouse.com/teachers

Library of Congress Cataloging-in-Publication Data
Mayer, Melody.
Have to have it : a nannies novel / by Melody Mayer.— 1st ed.
p. cm.
Summary: Kylie, Esme, and Lydia continue their friendship as they work
in Hollywood as nannies and try to make some decisions about the boys
in their lives.
ISBN-13: 978-0-385-73351-9 (trade pbk.) — ISBN-13: 978-0-385-90366-0 (glb. edition)
ISBN-10: 0-385-73351-8 (trade pbk.) — ISBN-10: 0-385-90366-9 (glb. edition)
[1. Nannies—Fiction. 2. Interpersonal relations—Fiction. 3. Friendship—Fiction.
4. Beverly Hills (Calif.)—Fiction.] I. Title.
PZ7.M4619Hav 2006
[Fic]—dc22
2005036531

The text of this book is set in 11.25-point Berkeley Oldstyle.
Printed in the United States of America
10 9 8 7 6 5 4 3 2 1
First Edition

In memory of my great-grandfather,
"Mr. Movies"

Have
to Have It

Kiley McCann

"You are just so . . . white," Jorge Valdez teased as Kiley McCann chewed her first bite of huevos rancheros *con camarones*—fried eggs on floury tortillas, with chiles and sautéed Pacific shrimp—definitely the most interesting thing she'd ever had for breakfast. It was so far afield from her usual Cream of Wheat or a toasted English muffin with jelly.

"I'm *what?*" Kiley managed to sputter through her mouthful of eggs.

"You should see your face," Jorge went on, grinning. "It's priceless. Like a little girl on Christmas morning who just got a pony."

"A little *white* girl," Kiley corrected, sipping some orange juice and digging in for another bite. She knew he was teasing her, and didn't really mind at all. "What can I tell you? It's the best thing I ever tasted."

Kiley sipped her coffee and looked around Bettina's Café, which, according to Jorge, was the best breakfast joint in all of Echo Park. This Los Angeles neighborhood was known for its high crime rate, gangs, and drive-by shootings. *Español* was the lingua franca, and Kiley was the only white person in the place.

Bettina's might as well have been ten thousand light-years from Kiley's birthplace of La Crosse, Wisconsin—home of the world's largest six-pack. Her father worked at the La Crosse Brewery and drank too much. Her mother was a waitress who was prone to panic attacks. The closest they'd ever come in their gustatory experience to what she was experiencing at the moment was the Taco Bell next to the La Crosse Wal-Mart.

"So, it's good, eh?" Jorge sat across from Kiley in one of Bettina's utilitarian orange plastic chairs. He was seventeen, just like Kiley. Skinny, of medium height with surprisingly broad shoulders, Jorge had very high cheekbones and amazing deep-set eyes the color of light just before dawn. They shone with intelligence and kindness. He had certainly been kind to Kiley, considering he barely knew her. In fact, she'd met him for the first time the night before.

Now she was living with him.

Kinda.

To make matters even more surreal, her maybe-in-the-process-of-becoming-boyfriend, Tom Chappelle, had been the one who dropped her off at Jorge's house. Tom had seemed to size Jorge up, as if Jorge could turn out to be a romantic rival. Or maybe that was all Kiley's imagination; the way she wanted things to be. Tom was a freaking *model,* for God's sake. A famous model. And she was plain old Kiley McCann from Wisconsin. Pretty much on a daily basis she asked herself why Tom was dating her. His former girlfriend, she knew, was a supermodel like him.

From the moment Kiley had met Tom at the Hotel Bel-Air, all she could think of was Brad Pitt in *Thelma and Louise,* a movie from the eighties that she and her mother loved to rent and watch together. Brad Pitt in that movie was the sexiest guy on the planet. That was one of the few things upon which she and her mom agreed.

Tom's face and torso were currently gracing dozens of billboards all over Los Angeles, including a fifty-foot one directly above Sunset Boulevard in Hollywood, where he wore nothing but Calvin Klein boxers and an "I want you" look on his chiseled face. Thousands—hundreds of thousands!—of Los Angelenas were currently lusting after the blond-haired billboard guy in the blue boxers. That makeup-free, not-exactly-skinny Kiley McCann from La Crosse, Wisconsin, was with him was bizarre. That Tom would consider any other guy competition was insane.

It has to be all in my imagination, Kiley decided.

Her eyes went to Jorge as she swallowed a bite of shrimp. He wasn't nearly in Tom's league in the looks department. Still, there was just something about this guy. A presence. A stillness in the midst of the chaotic restaurant. She could definitely see why girls would be attracted to him. Not *her,* of course.

"You're looking at me like you're about to eat me for breakfast," he commented.

Kiley blushed. "Oh, sorry. Lost in thought." She took

another bite of huevos rancheros. "This is so good. Can we come back for lunch?"

She was gratified when he nodded. She looked around the restaurant. The place was small—no more than ten tables—and seemed even smaller because of how jammed it was. The digital Dos Equis clock read 10:30 a.m., but an overflow crowd was enjoying a late breakfast. There were lots of families and couples, their flirting and joking a loud Spanish counterpart to the salsa-format radio station piped through the sound system. As for the décor, Bettina's decorations were unlike any that Kiley had ever seen in an eating establishment: the walls were plastered with posters for soccer teams like Real Madrid, while twinkling Christmas lights hung at uneven intervals across the pale green walls.

Kiley had a sudden realization: she and Jorge were the only two people in the place speaking English. Jorge seemed to pick up on her thoughts.

"So you're a gringa." He shrugged and took a sip of *horchata*—a delicious cold rice-based drink he'd made Kiley taste. "They do let white people in here," he said with a straight face. "Then we beat the hell out of them and rob them."

Kiley gulped. With her auburn hair in a messy ponytail and her fresh-scrubbed face, no-name jeans, and a La Crosse High School T-shirt, she knew that she was conspicuous. As a girl, she was an easy mark. Not that she had anything for anyone to steal.

"Hey, I'm teasing you," Jorge said. "Don't worry so much."

"I wasn't," Kiley fibbed.

How she had come to this moment seemed dreamlike, since three weeks ago she had been an ordinary girl in ordinary La Crosse, Wisconsin.

Things started to change when she entered a reality-TV show competition to become the live-in nanny for rock superstar Platinum's three kids. She had no real interest in the job, or in becoming a reality-show celebrity, but she did have a huge motivation to become a California resident. It was the first step in a master plan that would allow her to apply to the Scripps Institution of Oceanography and be eligible for in-state tuition. Scripps was her dream school, but the cost if you were out of state was out of sight. As for a college fund, Kiley had none. Neither of her parents had attended college, and they hadn't given much thought to planning for Kiley.

The miracle was, Kiley had actually ended up as nanny to Platinum's three kids.

Her dad always said that if something seemed too good to be true it probably was, and the disintegration of Kiley's dreams had begun twelve hours ago. Platinum, her boss, had been arrested. Her crime had been to leave drugs in a place where her children could get to them . . . and they had. Not only had Platinum been jailed for drug possession and child endangerment, but the kids—Serenity (age seven), Sid (age nine), and Bruce (age fourteen)—had been removed from the home by the California Department of Social Services. Calling the children's dad wasn't an option. Each had been fathered by a different guy; Platinum stayed absolutely mum about their identities. For that matter, so did the fathers. Almost as bad as the arrest itself was that Platinum's entire Bel Air estate had been declared a crime scene. Kiley had been given fifteen minutes to gather her belongings and get out.

It was only by the luckiest of breaks that one of Kiley's new friends in Los Angeles, another nanny named Esme Castaneda, had found a temporary place for Kiley to stay . . . back in Esme's old neighborhood of Echo Park, in the bungalow-style home of Esme's best friend, Jorge, and his family. Which was how Kiley had come to live with Jorge. Well, in Jorge's house, anyway.

She was overwhelmingly grateful to Jorge's parents, but still she knew she was living on borrowed time. It was only with great reluctance that Jeanne McCann had permitted Kiley to take the job with Platinum. If and when Mrs. McCann heard the news about Platinum, news that would surely be in the papers and on TV, she would demand that Kiley return to Wisconsin. And that, Kiley knew, would be that.

No California. No Scripps. *Adiós* and *hasta luego.*

Kiley had tried to head off the inevitable—even mailed a letter home that morning full of lies about how she was still living in Platinum's guesthouse and how Platinum would be home soon, begging her mother not to believe everything that was reported on TV. Now, with her head cleared by Bettina's strong coffee, Kiley realized what a feeble effort that had been. Her mom might not be highly educated, but she wasn't stupid.

Jorge swiped a napkin across his mouth. "It'll be okay, Kiley," he reassured her, then rubbed his chin thoughtfully. "I know. Think of yourself as an exchange student."

She laughed—a bit of gallows humor. "Stranger in a strange land, more like."

"Get used to it. If we're going to find you a job at La Verdad, you're going to have to. And bone up on your Spanish."

Kiley sighed. "I took French."

"Moi aussi," Jorge said, grinning. "But it's no use to either one of us around here." He sipped his drink again. "After this, we'll go see Geraldo, okay?"

Geraldo was the manager of La Verdad coffeehouse, a place that served coffee and *horchata* all day and light meals in the evening. Jorge and his group, the Latin Kings, sometimes performed there. If Kiley was going to stay in Los Angeles, she'd need a job, and that job was obviously not going to be as Platinum's nanny. Waitressing seemed her best and—in this town where eating out was an art form—possibly only option.

Kiley stirred her coffee. "I don't know why you're being so nice to me."

He draped an arm over the back of his chair and gave her a bemused look. "Why, people usually treat you like crap?"

She flushed. "No, it's just . . . Jorge, you barely know me."

"You're Esme's friend. Esme is my homegirl," he said simply. "Well, she used to be, anyway."

Something flitted across his face that Kiley couldn't quite read. Anger? Irritation? Disappointment?

"Are you mad at her for taking the nanny job in Bel Air?"

"She's smart and hardheaded and does what she wants to do." He sucked down the last of his *horchata*. "But this . . ." He swept his hand around the room. "These are her people. She doesn't have to give that up to make it out of the Echo."

"Is that what you think she's doing by working for the Goldhagens?" Kiley asked, surprised. "Giving it up?"

"You know her for what? Two weeks?" He wiped off his hands and tossed the blue paper napkin onto the table. "I don't expect you to understand, Kiley," he said, not unkindly. "It's not your world."

Well, that much was certainly true. Her world was—had been—as boring and colorless as a cold Wisconsin day when the snow was three days old and covered with a fine layer of soot. Still, she could understand a little about a person wanting to leave something behind. With every fiber of her girl-next-door being, Kiley did not want to go back to her old world.

Kiley studied Jorge for a moment. Interesting. Something about the way he said Esme's name, the syllables melting on his tongue like something delicious—chocolate, maybe. She wondered if Jorge loved Esme. If he did, she also wondered why Esme didn't love Jorge back. Surely his quiet self-confidence, brains, charm and—yes—sexiness couldn't be lost on her when they were so obvious to Kiley.

Of course, if Esme *did* see Jorge that way, it would complicate an already ridiculously complex situation. Not only did Esme have a boyfriend, a guy named Junior who was a gangbanger-turned-paramedic; she also had a *secret* boyfriend—Jonathan Goldhagen, the extremely hot son of her extremely rich and famous employer.

"Esme is my best friend," Jorge went on, as if reading Kiley's mind. "You know about Junior?"

Kiley nodded. She'd even met him.

"Junior is decent," Jorge continued, "I can't say he isn't. But he isn't good for Esme. All his status, everything he is, is tied up in the life."

"The life?" Kiley echoed.

"Gang life," Jorge clarified. "I know he's not a banger anymore. But still—"

"*¿Jorge, que hay, flaco? ¿Qué pasa contigo?*"

A pretty girl with a glistening waterfall of inky hair, who was wearing an orange halter top, orange miniskirt, and matching high-heeled orange pleather boots leaned a hip against their table. Her eyes flicked to Kiley.

"*No mucho, guapa,*" Jorge replied in Spanish at least as fluent as his English. "*Escuchas, quiero presentarte a una amiga, Kiley.*"

"*Mucho gusto, Kiley,*" the girl intoned, coolly looking Kiley over. "*Soy Blanca.*"

Even Kiley could understand that she'd just been introduced, and that the girl's name was Blanca.

"Hi," Kiley said.

Blanca's eyes flicked over Kiley again, then went back to Jorge. "You coming to Brenda's party tonight, Jorge?" This was in English, presumably for Kiley's benefit.

"I might," Jorge replied.

She leaned over, giving Jorge a full view of what Kiley could see was a burnt orange silk push-up bra. "I see you there, *ese.*" Kiley caught the promise of something more in her voice. Blanca straightened up, licked her lips, then swung her way out of the restaurant.

"She likes you," Kiley commented.

"She's sixteen, has a two-year-old daughter, and her ex-boyfriend is a banger. I don't have that much of a savior complex."

She had had her baby at age fourteen, Kiley mused. That sort of thing happened in La Crosse too, of course. But still, it seemed shocking. Kiley had enough trouble just trying to be a good nanny. She couldn't imagine actually being a *mother.*

"Anyway, I'm busy tonight," Jorge went on. "There's a rap slam at La Verdad. You'll be there training with one of the other waitresses."

"How do you know I'll get the job?"

Jorge shrugged. "Not a problem. Don't worry, I'll be your bodyguard."

Kiley laughed. "Have you always been this sweet?"

"Oh, my evil twin comes out now and then."

Kiley was about to say how much she doubted that when her cell vibrated in her pocket. "Excuse me," she told him, and dug it out. "Hello?"

"Kiley? It's Mom."

Mom. Who sounded anxious as hell.

"Hi, Mom!" Kiley tried to sound as upbeat and perky as possible. "How's everything at home?"

"I didn't call you to talk about home, Kiley. I called to talk about you."

Kiley swallowed hard. How much did her mom know? "Really?" she asked, hoping to buy herself some time.

"Don't play the innocent young lady. I raised you to be a lot of things, but a liar isn't one of them."

Kiley flinched. This was bad. Very, very bad. Obviously, her mom knew everything.

2

Esme Castaneda

"Hello, Junior?"

Esme lay back on her bed in the Goldhagens' guesthouse, her cell pressed against her right ear. She'd barely slept, so many thoughts running into other thoughts that it was impossible to calm her mind. At first her dreams had been weird; then they'd turned scary. She dreamed that Junior had died. When she awoke in a cold sweat, she was crying . . . until she remembered that Junior was going to be fine, that the drive-by bullet had only wounded his shoulder. He would be released from County General that day, if there were no complications.

It's guilt that made me have that dream, she thought. Guilt over being with Jonathan behind Junior's back.

She had Junior's hospital room number on some paper in her pocket. She dialed and got his extension.

"Yeah, baby?" His voice was strong, so much stronger than the night before when she'd visited him.

"How you doin'? You sounding better, *ese.*"

Funny, how easily she fell into the speech patterns of her youth, her barrio, when she talked to Junior. It was as if the girl who now lived in the guesthouse of a Bel Air estate had never left Echo Park.

"Hey, why wouldn't I be better?" Junior joked. "Lots of food, pretty nurses. The deputy mayor of L.A. had breakfast with me." She heard him chuckle. "He said I'm some kinda hero for taking that nine-one-one call for the gangs. Shit, if people like him did right, ain't no need for no gangs."

"You didn't tell him that!" she exclaimed.

"When you think I turned into a fool, *chica*?" he teased. She knew how he prided himself on being willing to take his ambulance to places that would make most paramedics—cops, too, for that matter—cringe. Whenever there was a gang shooting, or a horrific traffic accident in which kids were involved, or anything involving anyone identified as HIV-positive, Junior tried to be the first one on the scene.

"Anyway, *chica,* I'm good. Know the best part?"

"No. What?"

He chuckled. "Disability! I won't have to work until Christmas, I bet. Can fix up that Chevelle I bought from Victor, make it nice. Maybe you and me can go on a little trip. Las Vegas, maybe. Win us some major *dinero.*"

"Maybe," Esme told him, not wanting to commit to anything more.

"We talk about it later. I got a little *linda* nurse standing over my bed. Tell you what, I'll call you from my crib tonight, sound good?"

Esme nodded, even though Junior couldn't see. "Sounds good."

"Later, *esa.*"

" 'Sta luego."

She hung up, nibbling anxiously on her bottom lip. She was so relieved that Junior was better. But once he was home, she couldn't put off telling him about Jonathan. Just the thought of it made her sick to her stomach. She wasn't the kind of girl to cheat on her man. In fact, it was the first time in her life she'd ever done such a thing. She'd tried to break it off with her employer's son because she hated being such a cliché: the poor brown girl who fell hopelessly in love with the rich gringo. Love. Was she really in love with Jonathan? Or was it just lust that would play itself out for both of them? How could she possibly know? It was maddening! Was she really willing to break Junior's heart when she wasn't sure?

The message was on Esme's voice mail when she came out of the shower, water drops plopping onto the burnished hardwood floor of the bedroom of her guesthouse on the enormous Bel Air estate that belonged to her bosses, Steven and Diane Goldhagen. She unwound her long, thick raven hair from one of the plush French terry towels the Goldhagens had thoughtfully provided for her bathroom, wrapped another towel around her curvy, ochre-skinned body, and pressed the message button.

"Esme, Diane." Mrs. Goldhagen's voice was crisp and direct. "Please come up to the main house at ten-forty-five. Steven and I want to meet with you."

That was it. No hello, no goodbye. In a way, Esme wasn't surprised. Diane and Steven were used to giving orders. Steven was one of the most powerful men in Hollywood, the creator of a dozen or more classic television dramas over his storied career, including three that were currently on the air. Aggressively

13

casual, with a scruffy beard and the short haircut/baseball cap combo common to the balding Tinseltown elite, his usual jeans-and-T-shirt look belied a bank account that ventured high into nine figures. As for his wife, Diane, she was fifteen years younger, very thin, and quite pretty, with the sort of perfect blond hair that took tremendous upkeep at Raymond's salon to look as if it needed no upkeep at all.

The Goldhagens lived a life of opulence that Esme never could have imagined before she'd come to work for them. Their Bel Air home made the mansions she'd seen on TV look like bungalows in her old neighborhood of Echo Park. It had two guesthouses, a private tennis court, and a swimming pool, as well as a putting green. Their garage held eight vehicles—Steven had recently taken an interest in collecting sixties Chaparral race cars modified for street use, so there were three of those, plus a Hummer, a Lotus, a Beemer (Diane's chosen mode of trans-portation), an Audi (the car they usually asked Esme to drive), plus a new Prius that had been delivered only the day before. There was a driver on call from sunrise to three hours after sun-set, though he generally was engaged with chauffeuring Steven from one production set to another.

Diane was Steven's second wife—they had met when she was a production assistant on one of his TV projects. According to Jonathan, Steven's son from his first marriage, Hollywood was full of couples like them. The town attracted great-looking women who married less-than-average-looking men whose money and success were more powerful aphrodisiacs than a perfect Kumamoto oyster. Now that Diane and Steven were married, she didn't work anymore, unless you counted her beauty upkeep (a full-time job in and of itself) or her charity work, which ranged from holding honorary positions at the Arthritis Foundation and the Los Angeles Jewish Federation to organizing the charity banquet aboard the *Queen Mary* steamship that had been the culmination of the L.A. Fashion Bash, aka FAB—the trendy Los Angeles equivalent of New York's Fashion Week.

As Esme quickly towel-dried her hair, her stomach coiled into a tight knot of trepidation. Diane had caught her with Jonathan, in her guesthouse, which was strictly against the rules. The only saving grace, from Esme's point of view, was that they were not actually in bed. Since that was where she and Jonathan spent most of their time, she knew how easily this could have happened.

Well, there was no way out. She looked around the guesthouse. It had been built in the 1930s and featured huge exposed beams, beautiful hardwood floors, and many built-in California redwood fixtures. The furnishings were in keeping with the rustic theme—there was even a cast-iron stove in one corner of the living room for chilly winter nights. Outside was a classic veranda with two white wooden rocking chairs, two orange trees that shaded the parking area, and a basketball hoop. Esme wanted to make her mind into a camera and take it all in: the tranquility, the orange and freesia blossoms, whose scents wafted in from the garden outside her bedroom window. Because she realized there was a good-to-excellent chance that she was about to get fired.

3

Lydia Chandler

Lydia Chandler sat on the living room floor of her aunt's guest-house, wearing nothing more than the tiniest pair of La Perla pale pink French silk bikini panties that had come in one of the many unannounced packages that were regularly delivered to the house as a way to entice her famous aunt to wear, use, or consume something, and hopefully have her mention said product on the air. She could see the bedroom mirror from where she was sitting, and she liked what she saw: long, choppy blond hair, a deep tan, celery-colored eyes (well, she couldn't see those in her reflection, but she knew they were there), and a thin, almost waifish figure.

Hot underwear was definitely not her aunt's thing; all the better for Lydia. She took a sip of yesterday's coffee that she'd reheated in the kitchen microwave and opened the old-fashioned black Moleskine notebook in which she'd started a letter to her mother. She knew that her mom wouldn't get the letter until the next airdrop into the Amarakaire tribal village deep in the Amazon basin of South America, where her parents were currently medical missionaries and where Lydia herself had spent practically the entire last decade.

There really was no quicker way to communicate. Cell phone, e-mail, even telegraph—essentially impossible. There wasn't even a ham radio set. Outgoing mail had to be taken by skiff down the Rio Negro to start its journey to wherever. And the only time her mom could call was on her infrequent visits to Manaus, the nearest city large enough to have reliable phone service.

One good thing about her relationship with her mother, she thought as she wrote "Dear Mom": she could tell her mom anything and never get judged for it. Well, maybe not quite everything. For example, she could tell her mother that she now had a boyfriend, Billy Martin, who bore an uncanny resemblance to the guy who played Clark Kent on that TV show *Smallville*, even though her mom had never seen *Smallville* since there was no TV in the rain forest. But she couldn't tell her that while she had been ready to have sex with Billy practically from the night she met him, Billy was a romantic who wanted to wait until they "got to know each other better." Fact was, Lydia had been ready to join the ranks of the nonvirginal for years. However, all of those years had been spent living amongst nearly naked guys who had rotting brown teeth, were five feet tall, and carried spears.

Lydia nibbled on the end of her pen again. Maybe she *could* tell her mom how she felt about sex. It was possible; that was how cool her mom was. She definitely didn't have that kind of relationship with her father, which made her appreciate her mother that much more.

From the moment her parents had ruined her life by trading in their very, very rich and privileged Houston existence for a grass hut and roast monkey for dinner, Lydia had wanted nothing more than to get back to America. Especially in the last year or so, when her fantasies had been filled with boyfriends and first kisses and exactly where those kisses might lead. She'd even threatened to swim back. Then her aunt Kat had offered her a lifeline—the chance to come to Beverly Hills and be the nanny to her two children. Kat lived with her longtime partner, Anya Kuriakova, another former tennis champion. Their love affair and subsequent marriage in Massachusetts had been sensational tabloid fodder, but after some Ama fertility rituals Lydia had observed, it all seemed rather quaint. Her aunt was gay. So what? All that really mattered to Lydia was that they lived in an actual zip code. That the zip code was 90210—Beverly Hills—was karmic icing on the cake.

> Dear Mom,
>   Greetings from Beverly Hills!
>   How are you and Dad? How is Balagak, the shaman? I have not been following the weather— I guess I could do it on Kat's computer, but I've barely figured out how to set up an account on Yahoo for e-mail. Most of the time, I don't even remember to check it! I would give you the address, but I know there is no way you

could even e-mail. You seem so far away. I guess that's because you are.

So, about my job. I hate to tell you this, but your sister Kat's partner and the kids are a mess. I sort of remember Anya from when she and Kat were both on the tennis circuit, and I remember her as nice. What the hell did I know? Mom, she is like this tennis Nazi. She has totally ruined Martina and Jimmy. Neither of them knows how to have any fun; basically they are scared of their shadows. Actually, they're afraid of Anya—Momma Anya, as they call her. She is so controlling that she makes a list for me every morning of my duties with the kids, and it's so detailed that she practically tells me when they're allowed and not allowed to take a crap. Anya has the kids thinking they are allergic to anything with milk—I have to tell you that I like fresh goat milk a LOT better than the pasteurized and homogenized white stuff that you buy here in the supermarket—but the fact is they're not allergic at all. When I tried to tell Anya this she was ready to dump a school of piranhas in the pool and then toss me in afterward. She is not very happy with me right now, probably because I'm trying to bring some F-U-N into her kids' lives.

Los Angeles is fabulous. You can do anything or get anything, any time you want it. You want to go to the movies at midnight? No problem. Eat

Chinese food at four in the morning? Everything is for sale, and I do mean everything. All it takes is money to buy it. Okay, I can hear your voice in my head reminding me about the waste and the evils of a consumer-based culture. But Mom, I love it.

I've made a couple of good friends. We met at the Brentwood Hills Country Club, and both of them are nannies like me. Esme is a great girl from a really poor section of Los Angeles. She's the nanny to this big Hollywood producer who makes a lot of television shows. I like her. She doesn't take shit from anyone. She does tattoos of her own original designs. I'm thinking about getting one, maybe a huge gecko on my back. My other friend is Kiley, who works for the rock star Platinum. Remember you used to play her CDs when we still lived in Houston? Anyway, Platinum got arrested for drug possession, so Kiley's situation is a little dicey.

You wouldn't believe all the kids who do drugs here. It's funny, I know that the Amas blow only God knows what up their noses, but their kids know not to do it until the elders decide they are ready. In Los Angeles, there really aren't any elders looking out for anyone. For me that's great. But for kids . . . not so great.

Well, write to me when you get a chance. I know that pens and paper are precious. So sorry I missed your phone call when you were in Manaus! I miss you

so much, Mom. Say hi to Dad and to Balagak.
I'll write to you again soon.

Love,

Lydia

She signed her name in a schoolgirly scrawl, probably because when she'd lived in the rain forest, she hadn't had a
whole lot of practice. Then she realized that she had neither envelope nor stamps. Well, she'd just have to look up at the main
house—it shouldn't be too hard. She hadn't seen Anya all
morning. That might be a good thing, since undoubtedly Anya
was still pissed off at her from the day before.

Lydia winced, recalling the confrontation. Ever since she'd
arrived in paradise, she'd been raiding the moms' closets and
drawers. There, she'd hit the mother lode: cashmere tank tops,
heaps of candy-colored Juicy Couture sweat suits, several train
cases brimming with Nars and Dior lip gloss palettes, dozens of
Swarovski crystal–crusted bangles. They had way more stuff
than they could ever use, and Lydia had shown up in Los Angeles with nothing more than the clothes on her back.

She had assumed that Anya was clueless to what was being
borrowed. Turned out her aunt's partner had been keeping a
detailed list, which she'd yanked from her purse quicker than a
cobra strikes a river rat. Anya's plan (she'd informed Lydia with
far too much relish) was to present this inventory to Kat when
Kat returned from her business trip.

Whatever. Lydia felt certain she could make her aunt understand her plight. A girl couldn't walk around Los Angeles naked,
after all. Not that it would have disturbed Lydia all that much

(except in the fashion sense—she adored designer clothes), since she was utterly comfy in her own skin.

But think of all the boys she'd get hot and bothered and then have to disappoint.

Hell. Kat would understand on a humanitarian basis alone.

4

"So . . . Mom! Good to hear from you," Kiley cried, trying to sound as cheerful and carefree as possible. It came off false and she knew it. "What's up?"

"What's up?" Jeanne McCann cried. "What's *up*? Your boss got arrested for drugs and they took her kids away. It was all over *The Today Show* this morning!"

"*Really?*" Kiley played dumb.

"Stop that right now, Kiley. I was not born yesterday. When were you planning to tell us?" her mother demanded.

"I just wrote you a letter about it." Kiley tried to keep her voice calm, and unconsciously crossed her fingers before adding a lie. "You don't have to worry, Mom. It's a big publicity stunt."

"Kiley." Kiley winced. She could hear the disappointment in her mother's voice. "They made her house a crime scene."

Think, Kiley, think.

Kiley tried, but someone turned up the radio station on the sound system. She had to raise her voice over the music.

"Uh . . . I bet it was really exaggerated on TV, Mom."

"Where are you right now, Kiley?" her mother demanded. "And what is that *crazy music*?"

"I'm . . . in a coffee shop. Having . . . coffee." She nibbled nervously on her lower lip. Across the table, Jorge offered a sympathetic look. "I stayed with one of my friends last night."

"Which friend?"

"Another nanny. But don't worry," Kiley assured her mother. "I'll be back at Platinum's in a couple of days."

"Are you sure?"

"Of course, Mom. Really, there is totally nothing to worry about."

Her mother sighed. "It looked really bad on TV, Kiley. Three of my friends have called me because they saw it too. Everyone knows you were working for that crazy woman."

"I'm *still* working for her," Kiley insisted. "This whole thing will blow over."

"What will you do if it doesn't? Where will you live? Who is going to look out for you? Kiley? Are you there? *Are you there?*" Her mother's voice rose with each question.

"Breathe, Mom," Kiley counseled. "In, out, in, out. I promise you, I'm fine."

Kiley could hear her mother panting for air through the phone. She was hit by a pang of guilt. Her father was too distracted by the local tavern to pay much attention to what was going on with her mom and her panic attacks. He wasn't the most nurturing of people, even in the best of circumstances, claiming it was his wife's own fault for refusing to take any kind of medication for her "nervous condition." Kiley's mom had been raised a Christian Scientist, and didn't believe in pharmaceutical intervention. Sometimes kava root and passionflower herbs helped her, and sometimes they didn't. Kiley knew she was the only one who could consistently talk her mom down when her panic spiraled out of control. Kiley also knew that this particular downward spiral was all her fault.

"I'm really sorry, Mom," Kiley said softly. "I should have called you."

"Yes, you should have," her mother said. "I let you stay in California by yourself because I trusted you. To see this on TV before I heard it from you—it's terrible, Kiley."

Kiley flushed, ashamed. "I knew you'd worry—"

"When I get my break at the diner I'm walking down to La Crosse Travel and buying you a plane ticket home."

Now it was Kiley's turn to panic. "No! Mom, you can't!"

"*Home,* Kiley," her mother insisted. "I'll call and tell you which flight."

"But—"

"But nothing. It's time you faced reality, Kiley. It's over."

5

Esme went to her chest of drawers—eighty years old, it had been purchased by Cary Grant when he'd owned the estate—and threw on a black long-sleeved tee from an outlet mall (it had a couple of holes, but whatever) and a faded pair of Blue Asphalt jeans from ninth grade, along with a battered pair of black Old Navy flip-flops. No makeup, no lip gloss, no nothing.

I'm the nanny, she reasoned. *My job is to look after the kids, not to look good. All the Wet 'n' Wild lip gloss in the world isn't going to change whether or not they fire me.*

Esme sent up a little prayer: Por favor, *don't let that happen.*

She'd been so ambivalent about taking the job. But now, after two weeks, she felt panicky at the idea of losing it. She'd been offered the gig when Diane had come back from a charity trip to Colombia with an unanticipated gift for her husband—identical twin girls she'd adopted in Cali. Their real names were

Isabella and Juana, but Diane had renamed them Easton and Weston, and they were identical except for a heart-shaped beauty mark on Weston's cheek. Diane didn't speak Spanish, nor did the girls speak English. Since Esme's mom and dad worked off the books as the Goldhagens' housekeeper and groundskeeper, Diane had turned to Esme's mother for help. Mrs. Castaneda had suggested Esme. That had been good enough for Diane to offer Esme a trial employment period as her nanny.

"Esme? You in here?"

Esme's heart raced when she heard Jonathan call her from the front door. A young actor who'd gotten excellent reviews in a well-received if not well-attended independent feature called *Tiger Eyes,* he'd taken an immediate liking to Esme. More than a liking. Though she'd fought it, she'd taken more than a liking to him too. He was amazing-looking: short brown hair, startling blue eyes, and the rangy build of a born athlete. Easily six foot one, he had charm, manners, and a graceful ease about him, as well as a sensitivity that Esme had never encountered in the macho guys of Echo Park. If she drew a circle that was Jonathan, and then drew another circle that was Junior, her ex-gang-leader boyfriend from the Echo, those circles wouldn't intersect at all. They were *that* different from each other.

No, that wasn't entirely true, Esme realized. They were both good people. In fact, maybe Junior was even a *better* person. At least he had been tested in his life. Jonathan had always had it easy.

"I'll be out in a minute!" she called back to him.

She peeked out of her bedroom door and caught his eye.

He'd evidently come straight from the tennis court, since he wore a tennis shirt, warm-up pants, and carried three Head racquets under his right arm.

Two minutes later, Esme stepped outside, having rebrushed her hair into glossy perfection and traded in her ratty T-shirt for a blue one she'd found at a really trendy thrift store in Hollywood. It fitted her just so, and she left the first three buttons unbuttoned to hint at her curves. She had her pride, after all. She found him sitting on the stone bench by the far end of Esme's parking area—an area that doubled as the estate's basketball court.

"I have to go meet your parents," she told him as she took a seat. "Diane called."

"Ah yes, the royal summons," he mocked, then brushed a lock of hair from her cheek. "And she's not my parent."

Esme checked her Timex. She had ten minutes. "Well, whatever she is, she hired me and I'd prefer not to be late when she fires me."

"I've got some information that I think you'll appreciate," he reported.

"I'll take anything." She rubbed her burning eyes, musing on the night before. First, Diane had caught her and Jonathan in her guesthouse. Esme had been sure that she'd be fired on the spot. But Jonathan had stuck up for her and Diane had retreated, warning that she would consult with Steven and discuss the entire matter with Esme the next day.

Then Esme had gotten a call from her friend Lydia Chandler—another nanny whom she'd met at the Brentwood Hills Country Club—with the news about Kiley and Platinum. The two of them had rushed to help Kiley; Esme had had the sudden brainstorm to enlist her good friend Jorge in the effort to keep Kiley from going straight back to Wisconsin. That effort had been successful, and Jorge had immediately invited Kiley to sleep in his brother's empty bedroom at his family's Echo Park bungalow. Esme hadn't gotten back to the guesthouse until five and hadn't gotten to sleep until six. That sleep had been fitful. Though Diane hadn't fired her the night before, there was a good chance that the guillotine would drop that morning.

God, what would her parents say if that happened? Even worse, would spiteful Diane fire them, too, for what their daughter had done?

"Your job is safe. I talked to my dad at breakfast."

Esme grabbed his hand. "Really?"

He nodded. "Before Diane came down."

Esme felt her body sag with relief. "I was so worried. . . ."

"I know." He put a comforting arm around her. "I should warn you, though. You're about to get clocked with some pretty strict rules."

"Such as?"

He moved his arm and ran his hand impatiently through his hair. "Like middle school shit. Here on the sacred family grounds, you and I are strictly friends. No public displays of affection. Definitely no visits to your guesthouse."

Esme swept her damp hair off her face. It wasn't as if this was a shock. After all, those were a stricter variation on the rules she'd shattered in the first place.

"To quote my father," Jonathan continued, " 'What you do in the outside world is your own business, Jonathan. But I'd feel more comfortable if the two of you weren't alone on the property. And I *know* you want to make me comfortable.' "

"Right," Esme agreed. What else could she do? A ruby-throated hummingbird flitted down from the tulip tree behind them and hovered motionless in the air not five feet from them, outlined perfectly against the crystalline blue sky. Esme realized how quiet it was—so quiet that she could hear the flitting of the bird's wings.

"It's never this quiet in the Echo," she said softly, once the bird had flown off in search of more nectar. Esme had read about hummingbirds. They had to eat and eat and eat, because of how much energy they consumed in flight. Sometimes she felt as if she had to run and run, just to stay ahead of her past, maybe even ahead of her destiny.

It was so easy for someone like Jonathan. It would never, ever be easy for her.

"So, what do you think?" he pressed. "Can you live with that?"

"Sure," she replied, forcing a coolness that she didn't feel.

Evidently he could live with it, or he wouldn't be presenting it to her now. So what if there was this electricity between them? If he could keep his hands off her, she could damn well keep her hands off him. He was just a *guy*.

I am such a fraud, she thought. Even at that very moment, it was everything she could do to keep her hands off him, her lips away from his. Could she trust herself to live by her boss's rules, or would it just be too much torture? What about Junior? Where did he fit into the scheme of things?

"Sure?" Jonathan echoed, sounding hurt. "I don't understand you, Esme Castaneda. Last night, you told me you didn't want to skulk around in secret. I got right in my stepmother's face about you. I'm ready to go public, I told you that. We don't have to hide in the guesthouse. Wherever you want to go—

Viper Room, Geisha House, the Derby, goddamn Spago, even though no one in there is under fifty—if that's what you want, just tell me. *Just say where.*"

God, she was so confused. What if she said: "Let's hop in a Chaparral and go to House of Blues." How would it work? During the day she'd be the hired help, and at night she'd be his girlfriend? She rubbed the tight spot between her eyes. She had no time to figure this out; she had to go meet Diane.

Why can't I be like Lydia? Lydia would say go for it, sleep with Jonathan and sleep with Junior, and keep your mouth shut about both of them. But I'm not like Lydia, and I never will be.

She checked her watch again: 10:43. If she was going to make it to the big house on time, she'd have to hurry.

She rose. "Right now, I've got to go talk to your dad and Diane."

He got up too. "Yeah, whatever."

Jonathan was obviously bummed, but he had to give her time. She wanted to do the right thing. But for the life of her, Esme couldn't figure out what that right thing was.

For all the time that Esme had been working for the Goldhagens, she'd never once set foot in Steven's home office. To get to it, she had to enter the main house through the rear entrance; go through the ultramodern kitchen sporting a new five-hundred-dollar Gaggia Classic espresso machine; cross a game room with original arcade versions of Pac-Man and Donkey Kong, several Xbox 360s, and a professional British snooker table; and then continue through the meeting room, which featured a long teak table with a dozen high-backed black leather chairs, four white boards along the far wall for note-taking, six

Sony VAIO Notebooks, a video-conferencing PC, DVD players, and a huge Sony plasma monitor that hung on the north wall. Evidently, Steven didn't have to leave his estate in order to conduct his business, though Esme knew he had a suite of offices that triangulated perfectly between the Endeavor, William Morris, and CAA talent agency headquarters.

When she reached Steven's office, she knocked on the black glass double doors. An efficient beep was her signal to push the doors open; Steven and Diane were at the far end, huddled behind Steven's desk, eyes on a flat-screen computer monitor. Steven waved Esme to one of the black barstools that were set not far from his gunmetal desk.

With nothing else to do, Esme peered around the room. Everything—the triple-coated, hand-painted walls, the ostrich-skin sofa, the in-wall speakers, the ubermodern lighting fixtures—was a variation on a theme in black and white. The only things that weren't black and white were posters of Steven's various television shows over the years (all of them were in black onyx frames, though) and a black trophy case containing three shelves of gilded Golden Globe and Emmy awards.

The whole effect was intimidating, and Esme couldn't get comfortable on the barstool. She thought maybe that was the whole point—that if Steven's visitor was uncomfortable, it would give Steven the power position on anything that was being discussed.

Finally Steven looked up. "Thanks for coming, Esme."

"Sure," Esme ventured. He was her boss—it wasn't as if she had a choice.

"Diane and I wanted to thank you for all your work with the children during FAB," he went on, putting his hands on his desk and leaning toward her. Diane mirrored the gesture with her French-manicured hands, which gave Esme the distinctly uncomfortable sensation of being the subject of an interrogation.

"It was fun."

"We've been talking this morning, and we've—I've—talked with Jonathan as well. Has he spoken with you?"

Esme decided this was no time for fibs. "Yes. Just a little while ago. He came down to the guesthouse."

"For the last time," Diane stated flatly. "Did he make that clear?"

"Yes, he did."

Steven looked at her closely. "You need to give this some thought, Esme. We're very happy with your work. But I won't have your relationship with my son interfering with your duties to Easton and Weston."

Esme's chin jutted upward slightly. "I would not let that happen, sir."

"So we're all in agreement here?" Steven asked, folding his arms. He turned to his wife. "Diane?"

Diane nodded. "Just please understand that we are one hundred percent serious, Esme. If you break the rules again, we will have to let you go."

Esme felt like smacking the smug look off Diane's face. But she forced herself to keep her voice even, and pleasant. "I understand."

"Excellent." Diane smiled. "The girls love you, and we would hate to lose you. And now . . ." Diane tented her fingers, eyes shining. "We have a surprise for you."

Surprise? What surprise? Esme had had enough surprises in recent days to fill anyone's quota.

Diane came around the table, a sheaf of papers in her hand. She pushed them at Esme, who saw from the corny airplane-festooned logo that they were from some travel Web site. "We've decided that we're worn out by FAB," Diane reported. "We could use a vacation. We're going to take the kids to Jamaica."

"That's great!" Esme blurted. A few days of freedom from her job were exactly what she needed. "I'm sure you'll have a great time. I hear it's beautiful."

Steven smiled. "It is. And you're going to get to see for yourself. Our flight leaves at eight tomorrow morning. Make sure the girls are packed, okay?"

6

Lydia was met with a huge surprise when she let herself in the back door of the moms' house: her aunt Kat—who was supposed to be on the East Coast, prepping for her latest ESPN tennis reporting assignment—was sitting at the kitchen table with Anya.

Neither of them looked at all happy.

Not good. Anya had probably filled Kat in on the "borrowing" issue, as well as the "she sucks as a nanny" issue. Still, Lydia pasted a welcoming smile on her face—she'd learned from the Amas how to maneuver a power play: never let 'em see you sweat—and stepped into the state-of-the-art kitchen with its flowery, southwestern-style mosaic floor and stainless steel everything else.

Alfre, the moms' nutritionist, a radiantly healthy ex-hippie chick in suede Birkenstocks, was hard at work chopping raw scallions and red bell peppers on the counter. Lydia reasoned that this was a positive sign. If Alfre was on site for a talking-to, then the talking-to couldn't turn out to be too severe.

"Hey, Alfre," Lydia offered. "Whatever you're slicing sure smells delish."

"Raw veggies," Anya snapped with her thick Russian accent. "You have not eaten single raw veggie since you arrive from Amazon."

Well, okay, that was true, Lydia allowed mentally. But there was no need to make her into a criminal because she turned down the odd crudité.

Lydia suddenly flashed to a time in the rain forest when she'd been fishing alone. She'd been just about to climb back up the riverbank when she'd seen an angry tapir—a sort of anteater mutant—confronting her. This had been no joke, since the tapir had weighed about four hundred pounds. In that situation, the best defense can be a good offense. Lydia had flung her cane fishing pole at the beast, then had screamed and charged like a wild woman, figuring that if she stayed where she was on the log, she was a goner. The tapir had frozen in its spot for a split second, then turned its snouty face and bolted back into the jungle.

Two angry tapirs, minus the snouts, Lydia told herself as she took in the moms' scowls.

The best defense can be a good offense.

"Aunt Kat!" Lydia cried, as if just now noticing her in the room. She was also careful to emphasis the "aunt" part, as if unexpectedly seeing her aunt was perhaps the single most exciting thing that could happen to a girl. After all, blood was thicker than whatever it was Anya and Kat did under the sheets. At least, Lydia hoped it was.

"Alfre, would you excuse us?" Kat asked pointedly, without even so much as a look at Lydia.

Uh-oh. More not good. Alfre dismissed. Really, *really* not good.

"It's no problem, I've got to go to Whole Foods anyway," Alfre responded cheerfully. "We're out of organic sprouts."

Suck-up, Lydia thought. Alfre worked for these people. What was she going to say? No?

Lydia pulled down her cutoff Houston Oilers football jersey so that it covered every inch of midriff, and hitched up her cutoff shorts with the same goal in mind. These were the clothes in which she'd arrived, and she'd put them on just to be on the safe side. Never underestimate the power of nostalgia. "So, Aunt Kat. We didn't expect you home for a few days!"

Anya literally grabbed her partner's arm. "You see?" she cried. "She has responsibility of hamster! She acts like all is normal. All is not normal!"

Jeez, Lydia thought. *She probably has "Drama Queen" tattooed on both cheeks of her butt.*

Kat motioned for Lydia to take a seat at the far end of the table. Lydia did, noticing how tired her aunt looked; the disheveled expensive white silk Armani suit, the noticeable bags under her blue eyes. Since she'd gotten her new job as ESPN's chief women's tennis commentator, she'd been working very hard.

"Anya filled me in on the goings-on around here, Lydia."

Lydia played dumb. "Really?"

Her aunt's partner leaped to her feet and pointed a finger at Lydia. "You know, you know. You take daughter Martina for dessert. You make children eat bugs. Martina go belly dancing, I see her practice in room. You take clothes from Kat and my closet with no asking." She grabbed Kat's forearm again, this time in a death grip. "She give children *milk*!"

"Only to prove that they're not allergic," Lydia defended herself. "I mean, they might have been, but they're not anymore." She looked over at Kat. "Isn't it great that I found that out?"

No agreement was forthcoming. Instead, Lydia got an upbraiding from her aunt that went on for five minutes and covered everything from how Kat and Anya had done a favor for Lydia by bringing her out of the rain forest, to how Lydia was interfering with Kat and Anya's parental authority, to how Lydia was besmirching the Chandler family name with her unprofessional and downright dangerous behavior.

Lydia shook her choppy blond hair off her face and waited for the tirade to end. As she did, she made some quick calculations. Obviously, she was not going to be fired, probably because Kat still took pity on her for all those years in the rain forest with only air-dropped copies of *Cosmo* for company. She would have to bide her time on the reformation project for Martina, wherein she planned to help the plump, self-conscious, generally miserable ten-year-old to actually get a life. She'd have to figure out a way to get some decent clothes of her own instead of raiding the moms' closet. What about those upscale used clothing places she'd heard about? Maybe she could troll there and—

". . . nanny cam," Kat concluded.

Oops. Lydia had missed most of that, but anything that ended in "nanny cam" could not possibly be a positive development.

"Sorry?" Lydia asked, as pleasantly as possible.

"You heard," Anya accused. "You just don't like what you hear. Nanny cams. We need eyes in the back of head for you!"

Nanny cams. That had to be those closed-circuit television systems by which parents could keep an eye on their nannies' doings. Some parents hid the minuscule cameras in their children's Steiff animals. Her own aunt would do that to her?

"Gee, Aunt Kat, that's a little drastic," Lydia began.

"Not drastic enough!" Anya insisted, eyes blazing. "There must be confidences for what Lydia has done," she declared, after some further assassination of Lydia's character.

"Consequences, you mean," Kat corrected.

"Yes, yes," Anya agreed. "Consequences. In old Soviet Union when I was girl, we would go before committee."

"There are no committees here, but I can think of one thing in addition to the nanny cams that will show you how serious we are, Lydia," Kat mused. "It should also help you focus on your responsibilities." Kat rested her head on her hands and looked at Lydia. "How often does X drive you around?"

X was the moms' driver. A gay guy in his early twenties with exquisite taste in both clothes and friends (in fact, Lydia was in a hot relationship with his very hetero best friend, Billy Martin), he had gotten to be great buds with Lydia. She had taken advantage of his services not just to bring the children to various activities, but also as a way to get from point A to point B herself. It wasn't as if a girl could ride a bus to Los Feliz, nor could she have taken driver's ed in the Amazon.

"Some," Lydia ventured.

"Ha!" Anya barked. "I check mileage on BMW!"

Anya was keeping track of the mileage on the BMW, to see when Lydia was taking unauthorized trips? Jeez, Joseph Stalin had nothing on her.

Kat stood up. "Until the end of the summer, no unauthorized trips with our driver. If you're in the car with X, it's because we said you should be there."

Okay, this was definitely going to cramp her style. Without X, she was pretty much in a very well-heeled jail.

Anya took a list out of the pocket of her green velour pants dotted in artistically placed anchor appliqués. They were the sort of pants Lydia would have liberated from the moms' closet until recently. "Right now, you and children have appointment with local public library. I will drive you myself there to be sure children do not select comic books. Go get ready. Be at BMW in four minutes."

Kat nodded and Lydia realized that was that. Class dismissed. Well, at least she still had her job.

7

Kiley shoved her hands into the pockets of her jeans and forced herself to tell Esme and Lydia the horrible words she'd been thinking ever since she'd arrived at the Brentwood Hills Country Club: "This is probably the last time we'll be together."

They wound their way out of the kids' indoor play area that included a trampoline, a miniature golf course (complete with a giant windmill), a rock-climbing wall, a big-screen TV (high-def, of course), and a lifetime supply of LEGOs, video games, and Power Wheels. Ten feet ahead of them, Weston and Easton, wearing identical pleated Lilly Pulitzer skirts and bubble-gum pink polos, chugged along. They were mixed in with a gaggle of other kids, all part of the country club's "Nanny and Me" afternoon programming. Every kid carried a plastic golf putter.

Anya and Kat's children had wanted to be in the equivalent older kids' group, but Anya had been absolutely inflexible.

Instead, they had a private swimming lesson scheduled, and the private swimming lesson was what they'd attend. It gave Lydia some free time—she would meet them at the family pool in two hours.

"Hey, you never know," Esme tried to reassure her while still keeping a watchful eye on the twins.

"This time, I know," Kiley muttered. "My mom has me on a ten o'clock flight tomorrow morning back to La Crosse. Non-refundable."

Lydia offered a sympathetic smile. "Too bad that thing didn't work out at the coffeehouse with Esme's friend."

Kiley shrugged. "It wouldn't have mattered. My mom said I couldn't live in Echo Park." She shot Esme a guilty look. "No offense, Esme."

"No offense taken," Esme assured her.

"I don't see why we're just giving up, y'all," Lydia insisted. "We just need another good brainstorm session. Maybe I can find you another nanny job."

"I appreciate the offer," Kiley said, "but there isn't enough time. My mom wouldn't allow it, anyway. I think she's ruined for life on the idea of me being a nanny. God, it's so ironic. Here I am at the first day of Nanny and Me—a nanny with no kids to nanny for, because they're under state protection."

Nanny and Me was one of the country club's most popular programs. Many of the members were parents of kids under the age of nine, and many of those parents worked full-time and/or did charity work full-time and/or were simply too busy with paraffin pedis, shopping sprees, or cheating on a spouse in a bungalow at the Beverly Hills Hotel. So the country club offered Nanny and Me, where special counselors organized activities for the children and their nannies. It seemed as though all the country club kids had nannies—many had more than one, with the second nanny to fill in on weekends and days off. Sometimes a third nanny covered nights.

Today was the first day of this season's Nanny and Me; Kiley was impressed by the turnout. There were upwards of three dozen nannies—she heard accents from France, England, the American South, Jamaica, and the Far East—shepherding twice that many young children.

In a way, being there was painful. The whole day had been painful, in fact, and not just because her mother had ordered her to come home. Even the skimpy helping hand that Jorge had offered, the possibility of her waitressing at La Verdad coffeehouse, had been ripped asunder by reality. Kiley had hoped against hope that if she had a job, her mother would relent. But it turned out that La Verdad had no job openings. Jorge tried to cajole Geraldo, but it was no use. In the end, he was as disappointed as she was.

They'd just been leaving La Verdad when Kiley had gotten the call from Esme—did she want to come to the country club? At first Kiley had demurred; then she'd decided that they'd probably not even let her through the iron gate. But Esme had insisted, and asked Jorge to drop Kiley at the country club. He'd agreed, since he'd ordered some books from Dutton's bookstore in Brentwood, which wasn't all that far away from the club. Kiley realized she had nothing better to do, so she took Esme up on her offer.

To her surprise, she had no problem getting into the club—the skinny security guard with the bleached blond hair recognized her and waved her through. She met Esme and Lydia in the activity center with the kids. The first thing she noticed was that Lydia wasn't decked out in her aunt's "borrowed" couture duds. Instead, she was in her old ratty Houston Oilers jersey and cutoffs that she'd brought back from the Amazon. Lydia quickly explained how she'd been busted by the moms and how her closet-raiding days were a thing of the past. As for Esme, this would be her first and last day at Nanny and Me for a while, since she was going with the Goldhagens on a snap vacation to Jamaica the next morning.

Kiley bumped a hip softly into Esme's as they walked past the grass tennis courts, one of the few such facilities in Los Angeles. "You didn't say exactly who else was going to Jamaica, you know."

"In other words, is Jonathan going?" Lydia translated. "She didn't tell me, either."

"The answer is no," Esme said. "Just Steven, Diane, the twins, and me. They're meeting another family down there. The Silversteins or something like that. It's just as well because this morning Jonathan and I—"

She stopped midsentence, because the twins were gleefully launching themselves into mud puddles that had been left by the tennis court watering system. "Weston! *¡Por favor, no más d'eso!*"

"*¿Por qué no?*" Weston asked, hands on nonexistent hips. "*¡Es más diversión que esta actividad estúpida!*"

Esme cracked up.

"What did she say?" Kiley asked.

"Why should I stop?" Esme translated. "It's more fun than this stupid thing we're going to do."

Kiley laughed. "They're so cute."

Esme rolled her eyes. "Not all the time, believe me. Look at Easton." She pointed—Easton was giving chase to a big lizard, swinging her mini putter at it with malice aforethought. She gave up when the lizard scurried up one of the massive palm trees lining the walkway, but only after whacking the tree a few times for good measure.

"We used to eat those things in the rain forest," Lydia recalled. "They're really good if they're fried in fresh lard."

Kiley made a face. "Is there anything alive that you didn't eat down there?"

"People," Lydia mused. "But I can't speak for the Amas. Most of them have given up cannibalism, of course. But you'll always have your traditionalists." She looked over at Esme. "So what did you start to say about you and Jonathan?"

As they headed for the golf course, Esme brought them up to date on her new double-secret-probation status, which included no contact with the Goldhagens' son.

"They might as well put me in a burka so that nothing shows except my eyes," Esme complained. "Wouldn't want to tempt the royal prince."

Kiley was confused. "Wait, are you mad at Jonathan or something?"

"No," Esme mumbled.

"You say no but there's a yes in your voice," Kiley insisted.

Esme sighed and raked her long hair back with her fingers. "He says we can come out in the open and have a 'real relationship.' "

"So, that's what you wanted, girl," Lydia reminded her.

"How do we do that and at the same time pretend that we're nearly strangers when we're at home?" Esme queried.

Lydia shook her head. "See, now, I don't believe that's really what's holding you back."

Esme dead-eyed Lydia. "Oh, you know me better than I know me, is that it?"

Lydia stopped and pivoted toward Esme. "Maybe I do at the moment. You want this boy more than I want a no-limit Visa card, but you're afraid to admit how much you want him because it makes you feel all scared and vulnerable. How close to on the money would you call *that*?"

"Not to mention that you'd have to tell Junior everything," Kiley added, since she felt certain that Lydia was right.

Esme held up her palm. "Can we table this conversation? I'm supposed to be working."

The look on Esme's face made Kiley hold her tongue. It made her sad, too. It wasn't as if they could discuss it tomorrow, or the next day, or next week sometime, because Kiley would be back in La Crosse, filling out an application to serve deep-dish pepperoni pies at Pizza-Neatsa.

God, she was going to miss these two girls so much.

The grounds of the club golf course were normally off-limits to anyone who wasn't playing. On this exceptional Nanny and Me day, though, the welcome mat had been put out. There was literally a red carpet leading down the cobblestone path to the golf clubhouse, and a banner hoisted across the path announced: NANNY AND ME MINI-GOLF TOURNAMENT. TODAY! PUTTING GREEN CLOSED FROM 1:00 P.M. TO 3:00 P.M. NANNIES AND KIDS ONLY.

The moment they hit the red carpet, Easton and Weston charged ahead. The second they started to run, the pack of kids ran after them, laughing and shouting. A couple of little ones even dropped to the ground and rolled on their sides all the way to the bottom, nannies screaming and chasing after them, not wanting to be blamed for the damage done to clothes recently purchased at Fred Segal.

When they reached the putting green itself, Kiley saw that it had been decorated specially for the competition. A leaderboard had been erected, on which each of the kids' names had been painted, along with blank spots for their scores on eighteen holes. There was even a spectators' gallery, with bleachers and an overhang to protect it from the sun. Once all the nannies had taken charge of their kids, the head golf pro—forty years old with a hawkish nose and chiseled features; dark hair that was just beginning to gray at the temples; and tanned, muscled biceps straining his short-sleeved white golf shirt with the country club's logo embroidered in blue on the left-hand breast pocket—spoke into a wireless microphone attached to the collar of his shirt.

"Welcome, kids, nannies. I'm Oliver Sturman, head pro at the club and MC for today's event. Would the nannies please take seats in the bleachers? I'm sure you won't mind the break in the least. Golf staff members, please join up with two or three of the children. Thank you."

Lydia poked Kiley as they moved into bleacher seats with the other nannies. Meanwhile, eight attractive young men and women, all wearing the club's official white golf shirt, trotted out of the clubhouse. Each of them held a putter.

"Sturman," Lydia guffawed as she found a seat. "Sounds like Studman."

Esme, who sat on the other side of Kiley, peered around to Lydia. "Don't you ever stop thinking about sex?"

"In all honesty, rarely," Lydia confessed. "Well, of course, I do. When I think about shopping."

Kiley laughed. Even from where she sat, she could see a handsome young man—spiky, short dark hair, luscious caramel skin—speaking to Easton and Weston. They were obviously speaking Spanish, because the girls jabbered back as if this guy was their long-lost uncle. Then they turned to the bleachers with huge happy smiles, looking for Esme.

"Excuse me," Esme told Kiley and Lydia. "I think I'm being summoned. Save my seat."

"Nannies," Oliver Sturman intoned into his microphone, "we're pleased to present you with a welcome basket to this event, compliments of the club. You'll find those baskets directly under your seats."

Kiley reached under her seat. Sure enough, her hands touched a white wicker basket. It held everything that the nannies might need to be comfortable during what would evidently be a kids' putting competition: oversized J.Lo sunglasses, a butter yellow Lacoste sun hat, and a liter bottle of Badoit water from the Loire Valley in France, nestled in a special icy container—which also featured the club's logo—to keep it cold. There was also 40 SPF Kiehl's sunblock, Rosebud Salve, a jet black iPod Nano already filled with three hundred summer-centric songs (à la the Beach Boys), a copy of the latest editions of *People, Glamour,* and *Los Angeles* magazines, and a soft foam cushion to go between butt and seat.

Lydia pawed through her basket. "Screw this stuff, I need clothes. They couldn't throw in a designer T-shirt or two?" She held up the iPod. "Hmmm. Maybe I could sell this on eBay.

There's a notion. Maybe you could start an eBay business out of Jorge's house. I hear some people make serious money that way. You could stay in L.A.—"

"Not gonna happen," Kiley interrupted. "You don't know my mother." She smiled wanly. "Thanks for trying, though."

A few moments later, Esme rejoined them, and gave them the report on the assistant pro who had so captivated the twins. His name was Luis, he hailed from Costa Rica, and he was in America on a golf scholarship to Pepperdine University.

Lydia turned to check Luis out. He was attempting to teach Easton and Weston how to hold their putters properly, which was incredible, since a few minutes before, they had been more interested in swinging them at each other's heads.

"Marry him," she decreed. "No, wait, marriage is the last step before divorce. Have a torrid fling."

Esme shot Lydia one of her "if looks could kill" specials, which made Kiley's throat ache. No one in La Crosse was remotely like these girls. It hurt to be with them now, even, but in the best possible way.

As the golf pros were leading their junior charges out onto the putting green, Lydia watched Luis give some quick last-minute instructions to the twins. They appeared to hang on his every word as he dropped two golf balls to the manicured green, then pointed to a hole about ten feet away. He steadied Weston's hands on the putter, then helped her line up her shot.

"Okay," Kiley saw him say. "Do it."

Whap.

Weston struck the ball. It rolled thirty feet past the cup.

"Tiger Woods she isn't," Esme surmised.

"Who's Tiger—" Lydia started to ask, but was interrupted by someone at the base of the bleachers calling Kiley's name.

"Kiley! Yoo-hoo! Kiley!"

Kiley peered down into the crowd at the base of the bleachers. A tall, bone-thin woman with short dark hair, expensive-looking khakis, and a fitted oxford was practically jumping up and down, waving her hands as she shouted Kiley's name.

Lydia recognized her before Kiley did.

"Run for your lives, girls," she warned her friends. "Or call out the National Guard. It's the one and only Evelyn Bowers."

8

It was indeed Evelyn Bowers, who was supposed to be Lydia's inaugural client in her nascent nanny-placement business—Lydia's big make-scads-of-money scheme.

Lydia had, in fact, found Evelyn a nanny, but the nanny had turned out to be . . . strange. Still, from what Kiley knew, Evelyn Bowers was even stranger. Not only had she fired that nanny after less than a day on the job, she'd also gone off on Lydia, promising to bad-mouth her to every other mother in Los Angeles (a bit of an exaggeration since obviously she didn't know every mother in Los Angeles; but Evelyn was a publicist, and Kiley had quickly learned that the L.A. show business world was sort of like its own small town). This threat had pretty much killed Lydia's business before it had even gotten started.

So Kiley's question was, why did Evelyn want to talk to her? They'd met exactly one time, here at the country club. Evelyn had been wowed that Esme was working for the Goldhagens, and that Kiley was a nanny too. Lydia had done everything she could to underscore the impression that it had been she who'd gotten the girls their jobs.

"I suggest you go down there," Lydia advised. "Otherwise, she'll come up here, and that puts my life in danger."

"Fine. I'll talk to her." Kiley stood and edged her way to the bleacher stairs, then took them two at a time. As she did, Evelyn broke into a wide grin and pushed through the crowd to meet her.

"Kiley, it's great to see you again!" the woman said, taking both of Kiley's hands in hers as if they were long-lost friends. "How are you? How's every little thing?"

Kiley tugged her hands back. "Fine, Mrs. Bowers."

"Evelyn, please!" she insisted. "You're Platinum's nanny, right? Your friend-who-shall-go-nameless told me." Evelyn shot a look of pure loathing up the bleachers toward Lydia, who Kiley saw was looking everywhere but down at the two of them. But when Evelyn refocused on Kiley, she was as perky as ever.

Kiley cleared her throat. "Actually, I *was* working for Platinum but—"

Evelyn smacked an open palm against her own forehead. "Of course. How could I be so stupid! Platinum had that . . . *incident* last night. I read about it in the *Times* this morning." Evelyn's voice dropped at least fifty decibels. "A shame. Really. How terrible for those children. Did the arrest affect you personally in any way? I sincerely hope it didn't."

Kiley tried to hold back the bitterness she felt. "You could say it did, Mrs.—I mean, Evelyn. Her house is a crime scene. I'm not her nanny anymore. I'm going home to Wisconsin. Tomorrow. My mom already bought me a nonrefundable plane ticket.

So I would say so. Thanks for asking, though." She tilted her head toward the bleachers. "I should get back to my friends."

Kiley went to turn away, but Evelyn's lightning-fast hand clamped onto her forearm. "Kiley, wait. This . . . change in your circumstances. That means that you're . . . *available.*"

"In what sense?" Kiley asked warily.

Evelyn released Kiley's arm. "Well, it occurred to me when I read what had happened with Platinum—I really never thought the woman was stable—that if you were offered the right position as a nanny, you would be prepared to accept it immediately. More importantly, there would be no delay. You could start immediately." She grinned hugely. "In *that* sense."

Whoa. Was Evelyn offering her a job?

Kiley's mind raced. It was one thing to be living in Echo Park in a stranger's house and working as a waitress; it was quite another to be able to tell her mom that she'd secured an actual nanny position with someone who was far more stable than Platinum. She couldn't be certain, but her mother might actually be persuaded to let her stay in California under those circumstances.

Maybe. Please, God.

Evelyn was getting her Louis Vuitton checkbook out of her Kate Spade bag. "How much was the plane ticket, did you say?"

"I have no idea."

"Well, let's just say five hundred dollars and we'll work it out later." Evelyn scribbled the amount on her check and handed it to Kiley, curling Kiley's fingers around it. "There! I've left the payee blank for the moment. Why don't we take a walk up to the restaurant so I can interview you? If the interview works out—and I'm getting a *fantastic* vibe here—we'll call your mother together. You can either send this to her—we'll fill in her

53

name—or I can wire the money to her account in . . . where did you say she lives?"

Kiley was in a daze. "Wisconsin. La Crosse, Wisconsin."

"La Crosse," Evelyn repeated. "Well, I'm sure it's a fantastic place, and you were raised with all those salt-of-the-earth ethics that I would value so much in a nanny."

Aside from Dad being a drunk and Mom having daily panic attacks, sure. I'm just salt of the earth through and through.

Evelyn moved closer. "Let me level with you here, Kiley. I am desperate for a nanny." She folded both bony arms over her chest. "Your friend up there whose name I won't speak broke my heart. Do you realize that?"

"Well, I know you weren't happy with the nanny she—"

Evelyn put a forefinger to her lips. "Shhh. We can't talk about it, and we definitely can't talk about *her*. It's just too upsetting. This will be strictly between us, if we can reach an understanding. Am I making myself clear?"

"Sure," Kiley told her, thinking that she had nothing to lose.

As if the deal had already been struck, Evelyn stuck out her hand. Kiley had no choice but to shake it. "Okay," Evelyn told her, grasping Kiley's hand as if they were suddenly superglued to each other. "I've got a great idea. Let's go up to the restaurant and have some iced tea. And caviar on melba toast points. Do you like Russian caviar? I adore Arabian myself. My treat. We've got a lot to talk about."

9

"Come on, kid," Oliver Sturman pleaded with Easton. "You can do it. Just do the same thing you did before. One more time. Just put the ball in the hole."

He, Luis, and Esme were gathered around the little girl. Luis shook his head. "She doesn't speak English, she can't understand you."

"Ball!" Easton yelled up at them, her face red.

"Good girl!" Oliver exclaimed, giving Easton a big thumbs-up. He turned back to Luis. "Evidently she does speak some English, Luis."

"If you speak slowly, she'll understand a lot," Esme put in. "She's a very fast learner."

"Yeah, I can see that," Oliver agreed wryly. "Could you please tell her to just keep doing what's she doing?"

Luis traded a look with Esme. "I don't think this girl needs our advice, sir."

Esme would have to agree with that assessment. In the twenty minutes since Kiley had departed with Evelyn, the putting competition had fallen apart completely as Easton had become the center of attention. It had taken no more than a dozen putts for everyone within sight to realize that the little girl from Colombia had a natural talent for golf. No, more than a talent. She was weirdly, freakily, and unaccountably great at it.

Word of her ability had spread around the club like a brush fire in Topanga Canyon fueled by raging Santa Ana winds. Not only had all the nannies come down off the bleachers to gather around the green, the other young putting contestants were standing in a ragged semicircle just to watch Easton do her thing. Meanwhile, once T-Mobile Sidekicks and BlackBerries had been activated, golfers had abandoned the course and sped back in their golf carts to watch the prodigy, while other club members had hustled down from the clubhouse and the pool area.

The upshot was, there were now upwards of three hundred people crowded around the green, while exactly four people stood on the putting surface—the head pro, his assistant Luis, Esme, and diminutive Easton. As for Weston, she was off to the side of the crowd, huddled in Lydia's arms, babbling away in Spanish that Lydia didn't understand.

"*Tú estas lista por una otra?*" Esme asked Easton.

She nodded and pointed to the ground, indicating where she wanted the head pro to place a golf ball. Dutifully, he cleaned a ball on a towel monogrammed with the country club's crest and put it on the exact spot that Easton wanted.

"*Adónde?*" Easton asked. "Where?"

"*Número cinco,*" Luis suggested, motioning to a hole at the far end of the green. There was a fearsome dip about five feet from the cup; the cup was cut into the side of that dip. "Number five."

He leaned in toward the head pro. "That's basically an impossible putt, sir. Sixty-one feet from here, exactly. And she's got a heck of a break to the right in order to sink it."

"O-kay," Easton assured him in English. *"Yo estoy lista."*

"She's ready," Esme and Luis translated simultaneously.

As the gallery hushed, Easton grasped the putter just as Luis had instructed her, and leaned over the golf ball. She aimed, took two careful practice strokes behind the ball, then confidently struck it, keeping her gaze fixed on the spot where the ball had been before it rolled away instead of lifting her head to follow the ball's progress.

Everyone else watched the ball as it rolled toward the cup like a slow-speed cylindrical cruise missile locked on its target.

It was uncanny. Somehow the little girl intuitively read the break in the green perfectly and aimed well to the left of the cup; she'd taken into account the downward dip as well, and putted softly enough that the ball was barely moving when it reached the hill. At that point, gravity took over . . . until the golf ball dropped into the hole with a satisfying *ka-pluck*.

The crowd whooped and hollered in delight, and Luis smacked Esme on the back with excitement.

"Holy cow, this is amazing!" the head pro marveled as the cheering continued. Nannies with camera phones were snapping pictures of Easton, who didn't seem at all unmoored by the attention. "I've been keeping track. Inside of six feet, she hasn't missed. Six feet to twenty feet, she's hitting fifty percent. Over twenty feet, she's four out of sixteen, and all the ones she missed left easy tap-ins. I've never seen anything like it in my life."

His eyes went to Esme. "Are you the mom or the big sister?"

"The nanny," Esme retorted, bristling a bit. Obviously, this guy thought that because the children were Latina, and she was Latina, they had to be blood relatives. Wrong. "She's Steven and Diane Goldhagen's daughter. Remember? This is Nanny and Me."

The head pro started to apologize, but was interrupted by the second twin, Weston, who squirmed out of Lydia's grip and started running toward her sister.

"Ball! Ball!" she called, as she clearly wanted to share the spotlight. But the bizarre thing was, even though the girls were identical in every apparent way, Weston's golf was pretty much what you'd expect from a reasonably coordinated kindergartner—that is to say, pretty dreadful—while Easton's skill with the putter was nothing short of phenomenal.

"Sorry, duty calls," Lydia told the pro and Luis, hurrying after the little girl while Esme stayed with Easton.

"Me ball! Me ball!" Weston yelled. She picked the golf ball out of the cup and kept running. Finally, Lydia grabbed her and carried her back to her sister and Esme.

"*En dos minutos serás tu vuelta*, sweetie," Esme told Weston. "It will be your turn."

"No!" Weston yelled, as red-faced and angry as Esme had ever seen her. In fact, she hauled off and smacked Esme across the face with her tiny palm, to the shock of the gallery.

"*Eso era una cosa muy ala a hacer,*" Esme chided, struggling desperately to keep her cool, and reminding herself that the twins were under a lot of stress. "That was a very bad thing to do."

"*Te odio*, doodyhead!" she yelled at Esme, which made the nannies standing by the side of the green laugh uncomfortably. They might not know that "*Te odio*" meant "I hate you," but the "doodyhead" part came through loud and clear. It was funny, in a way, which was why the nannies were chuckling. But they also knew that but for the grace of God, it could have been them out there, with their kid making the scene.

"Weston, no!" Lydia admonished. "Esme, how about I take her for a walk up to the pool, and you can come meet us? I have to meet Jimmy and Martina up there in ten minutes anyway."

Before she responded, Esme couldn't help noticing the way Lydia kept looking back at Luis, the assistant golf pro. Her startling light green eyes gazed up at him from beneath her sooty lashes, and Luis seemed mesmerized. It was as if Lydia was advising Luis where he, as well as Esme, might be able to find her.

Fine. If Lydia wanted to flirt, that was her business.

Esme picked up Weston, walked away a few feet, and whispered in Spanish in the child's ear: "Go with Lydia to get Jimmy and Martina. Easton and I will come and meet you. Then you can pick whatever kind of ice cream you want at the snack bar. With whipped cream."

Yes. It was a bribe, using the thing that Weston loved most in the world—ice cream. She didn't like to bribe the kids. Sometimes, though, extraordinary times called for extraordinary measures.

When she came back to Easton, Lydia was introducing herself to Luis. It seemed as though Luis took an extra-long time shaking Lydia's outstretched hand.

"I'm Esme's friend," Lydia explained. "Lydia."

"Luis," he replied, still gazing into her eyes.

"Real nice," she drawled to Luis, giving him another flirty look. "To meet you, I mean."

Esme cleared her throat as loudly as possible, as a signal to Lydia to get going with Weston. Lydia got the hint. She took Weston's hand and they walked off together. Meanwhile, the head pro, Mr. Sturman, was placing another golf ball on the green for Easton to putt, seemingly oblivious to the embarrassing incident that had just taken place.

"I'd love to teach her myself," Sturman told Esme, "but I think the language barrier would be a problem. Why don't you suggest to Steven and Diane that Luis teach their daughter. No charge, as long as I can be one of her sponsors when she grows up? What do you say?"

Do you have any idea how rich her parents are? Esme thought. But it seemed impolite to say that.

"I don't think she'll need sponsors," she responded coolly.

"Hell, I just want to witness the process," Sturman marveled. "Can you imagine? It'll be like helping to make the next Michelle Wie." He clapped Luis on the shoulder. "You ready to take this on, you lucky son of a gun?"

"Yes, sir," Luis assured him with a broad grin. "Absolutely."

Sturman knelt by Easton's side and tried to give her a quick lesson on golf terminology—the green, the cup, the grip, the fairway, the course, and so on. As he did, Luis stood with Esme, and the crowd finally started to disperse.

"Which would you rather speak, Spanish or English?" he asked her.

"English. This is America."

"Works for me," the pro agreed. He barely had any accent at all. "You'll talk to her parents about lessons?"

"Definitely. But Easton won't be able to start right away.

We're going to Jamaica tomorrow. How about if they call you when we get back?"

"When will that be?"

"Friday. I think."

Luis dug a card out of his pocket and handed it to Esme. "Luis Josemaria de Castro. And no, I'm not related to Fidel."

Esme smiled again. This guy was not just very handsome, he was very, very charming.

"Esme? Yo soy casado de golf. Yo quisiera un helado, por favor." Easton tugged at Esme's sleeve.

"I'd suggest you get the girl an ice cream like she's asking for," Luis joked. "And if I could make one more suggestion . . ."

"Yes?"

Luis leaned close. "Give my phone number to your friend Lydia," he said, careful to keep his voice low.

"Are you planning to teach her golf, too?" Esme asked with an arched brow.

"Anything she wants to learn," he replied. *"Anything."*

10

"Just call the woman, Kiley. Get it over with."

Kiley was so nervous she felt as if she could have a panic attack worse than any of her mother's. She sat with Tom in his old pickup truck, which Tom had pulled up to the valet stand at the Velvet Margarita Cantina restaurant in Hollywood. He'd picked her up at the country club gate an hour before, and she'd babbled out the story of her amazing day—Evelyn Bowers homing in on her at the country club, their walk-and-talk interview around the grounds, and the conclusion of that interview at a white-tablecloth table on the rear brick patio of the huge country club restaurant, over caviar and toast points cut into perfect isosceles triangles.

"*Golden* caviar," Kiley had explained. "Evelyn said it's from the Arabian Sea and costs a mint. But she claimed that nothing was too good for the girl who was probably about to become her new nanny, because she considered the nanny a 'real member of the Bowers family.' "

The interview had ended successfully. Evelyn had offered Kiley the job and asked her to start the next morning. Kiley had been honest—she'd have to talk to her parents about it before she and Evelyn called them together, which Evelyn had found quaint but also a point in Kiley's favor. It indicated stability of personality, unlike Kiley's "so-called friend who shall go nameless." In fact, Evelyn had made it a condition of employment that Lydia not set foot on her property, nor telephone on the main house line, nor should Kiley speak to her on her cell phone from within the four walls of Evelyn's house. Kiley had acceded to these conditions. She really needed the job.

All of which was a dream come true, but for two things.

One, Lydia had filled her in on Evelyn and her children. They all belonged in a nuthouse. Two, there was no assurance at all that Jeanne McCann would give in. In fact, Kiley half-expected her mother to order her home—which was part of the reason they were sitting in Tom's pickup instead of heading into the restaurant. Kiley didn't know whether this would be their last meal together or something to truly celebrate.

Kiley looked down at her old Nokia cell phone. She'd already decided what she'd do if the answer was no—go back to Jorge's and spend her final night there. There had been a momentary thought about sleeping at Tom's, but Kiley had pushed it out of her mind. What if they ended up in bed together? That would confuse her too much, which was why she'd left her luggage at Jorge's.

"Okay, you're right, I just have to . . . do it," Kiley agreed. "Here goes."

She had the number at Vicki's (the diner/truck stop where her mom waitressed) on speed dial, because Jeanne McCann couldn't justify the cost of owning a cell. Remembering that made Kiley feel guilty all over again. Her mom had made so many sacrifices for her. It would make it so much easier if Kiley just went home, got a job for the rest of the summer, finished senior year at La Crosse High School, and then—

"Vicki's," a throaty voice answered.

Kiley recognized the voice of her mom's friend Angela, who'd twice had precancerous polyps removed from her throat yet still smoked a pack and a half a day. In the background, she could hear the din of the restaurant and the Toby Keith music that the owner liked to play over and over. Vicki's served a dinner special of roast beef, baked potatoes, corn and carrots, soup, and dessert for $7.95, and it was always jammed between four and eight in the evening.

"Hi, Angela, it's Kiley."

"Kiley, sweetheart!" Angela boomed. "Hey, I saw a thing about Platinum on the news, sweetie. We all did. She didn't force you to take drugs, did she?"

"No, Angela, nothing like that," Kiley assured her. "Is my mom there?"

"So what happened to her kids?" Angela pressed.

"Uh, I don't know yet for sure."

"I heard they took the kids away, Kiley. So Platinum is in rehab now? How well did you get to know her? What does she like to eat for breakfast?"

"I don't know, Angela, I never actually saw her at breakfast." Kiley shrugged helplessly at Tom. It was amazing. Everyone was fascinated by celebrities; that Kiley had actually lived with one for a while made her fascinating to Angela. "So . . . my mom? Is she around?"

"Oh, sure, honey. Hey, heard you're coming home. Hollywood ain't the place for a girl like you, sweetie. Hold on." Then Kiley heard Angela bellow, "Hey, Jeannie! It's Kiley! I'll get your tables!"

A few moments later, Kiley's mom's high-pitched voice came over the phone. "Kiley, sweetheart, are you okay? What's wrong?"

Trust her mom to assume that something was wrong.

"I'm fine, Mom."

"Did you lose your plane ticket? Is that it? I'll call La Crosse Travel and have them issue another one."

"No, Mom, I didn't lose my plane ticket, it's electronic. All I have to do is go to the airport," she said patiently. She could feel her hand sweating on the phone and wiped her right palm on her jeans. "I just wanted to tell you that something amazing happened."

She quickly filled her mother in on Evelyn Bowers, her quickie job interview, and the subsequent offer for a nanny job, starting the very next day. Then she spun the hell out of the situation—Evelyn Bowers was a "highly respected publicist" who "wasn't even in show business" and she'd "heard from numerous people" how "lovely" Evelyn's home was, and how "well-mannered" her kids were and couldn't she please, please, *please* stay and take the job?

Her mother sighed heavily. "Oh, Kiley, I don't know. Your plane ticket is nonrefundable. The whole time out there has been so aggravating for you. One thing after another after another. Maybe you just ought to cut your losses and come home."

"Don't worry at all about the ticket. Mrs. Bowers has already given me a check for that," Kiley said quickly. "That's how much she wants me to work for her."

Another sigh from her mom's end as the Toby Keith song ended.

"I just don't like the idea, Kiley."

If it called for groveling, fine. Kiley was prepared to grovel.

She tightened her grip on the phone. "Please, Mom. I want this so much. Mrs. Bowers said she'd call you herself tomorrow morning, you know, to introduce herself. I'll be on that call, too. She wants to make sure you're comfortable with this whole arrangement."

"But . . . what if it doesn't work out? What will you do then?"

"It *will* work out, Mom. I know it will."

"I don't know, Kiley. What if she turns out to be as weird as Platinum, or even weirder? So many things could go wrong. When I think of you all alone out there, working for some woman I've never met . . . I just don't know about this."

Kiley could hear her mother's voice soaring upward through the octaves, a sure sign that she was rounding the bend to a full-blown panic attack.

"It's okay, Mom," she soothed. "Really. It'll be fine. Remember when you said that you trusted me and that was why you were letting me stay in L.A. even though I'm still a minor?"

"Yes . . ."

Kiley could hear the doubt in her mother's voice. She pressed on.

"Remember how you told me you don't want me to be like you, scared of things?"

Silence. Then: "I did say that," her mother admitted softly.

"I know you meant it," Kiley insisted. "Well, I'm asking you to trust me, Mom. Just like you said you would. I'll do everything I can to make you comfortable with this. Mrs. Bowers is a publicist. Maybe . . . you can even meet her through a video hookup or something. Or . . . I know—maybe she'll pay for you to come out here to meet her!"

More silence. Kiley knew that this last suggestion was a shot in the dark and highly unlikely, but she crossed her fingers and sent up a silent prayer to whatever higher power might be involved in this sort of fateful decision anyway. *Please,* she prayed, knowing how stupid and even selfish it was to pray for this when she didn't pray for anything else, but doing it anyway. *Please, please, please. I deserve this, I deserve this, I deserve this, I de—*

"All right, Kiley."

Kiley's heart jumped.

"Did you just say . . . all right?"

"Yes, honey, I did. But Kiley, please have Mrs. Bowers call me in the morning. I won't rest easy until I hear her voice."

Kiley punched the air with glee. Tom rewarded this positive gesture with a huge smile.

"Absolutely, Mom," Kiley promised. "Thank you so much—"

"Kiley?"

Something about her mom's voice made Kiley feel as if she was seven years old again.

"Yeah, Mom?"

"Sweetheart, if you pull another stunt like the one you pulled with Platinum—and I know you know what I'm talking about—"

Kiley did. She'd lied terribly to her mother. She felt terrible about it, too.

"I'll be completely honest this time, Mom. Whatever happens. But nothing is going to happen," Kiley added hastily. "I swear it. This time things are going to work out."

"Yes. Well, life has a way of fouling up the best-laid plans, Kiley." Another heavy sigh as Toby Keith started singing again in the background. "I just hope I'm doing the right thing."

"You are, Mom. You definitely are!"

Kiley thanked her mother profusely, told her how much she loved her, and hung up. Then she threw herself into Tom's arms.

The sandy-haired valet shot them a dirty look when Tom, casually clad in Diesel denim, a Le Tigre polo, and chocolate brown suede Pumas, finally handed over the car keys. But since he also handed over a ten-dollar tip, the guy was somewhat mollified.

They pushed through the front door of the Velvet Margarita and were greeted by Mexican-tinged sights, sounds, and smells. Mariachis draped in fringed serapes milled around the red velvet booths, where the young, hip, and beautiful noshed on enchiladas and chimichangas. On the black velvet walls hung gaudy sombreros and candlelit caricatures of iconic celebrities: Elvis, Selena, and Madonna were the ones Kiley could instantly identify. Meanwhile, a deejay in a pink Day-Glo booth suspended from the two-story-high ceiling spun Mexican hip-hop—David Rolas, Crooked Stilo, Control Machete. Tom picked out a number of the tunes for Kiley as they waited for the maitre d' to seat them.

"How do you know Mexican hip-hop?" Kiley asked over the music.

"My friend La Daga," Tom explained, a protective hand on the small of Kiley's back, as a raucous, drunken group of guys made their way out of the restaurant. "The Dagger."

"That's a name?" Kiley asked.

"Exactly," Tom said. "His real name is Emmanuel, but he models under La Daga. We have the same agent. He's got that hot Latin thing going on; does lots of romance novel covers for Harlequin. Stuff like that. Great guy. Anyway, he does that for the bucks but really he's a rap artist. He's played all this stuff for me. In fact, he's the one who turned me on to this restaur—"

"Tom!"

Kiley squeezed her eyes shut, hoping that the voice she'd just heard calling to her date did not belong to the person she thought it belonged to.

"Tom, sweetheart!"

Damn. Her ears weren't lying.

Marym was making her way through the crowd toward them. The famous eighteen-year-old, raven-haired Israeli model wore a sandy wraparound sleeveless top over a floor-grazing BCBG cream skirt littered with embroidered golden leaves and looked, as usual, perfect. Kiley felt utterly provincial in her generic jeans and one of the few garments she'd acquired in L.A., a Forever 21 black-and-white-striped scoop-neck tee. She had met Marym when Tom had taken her to Marym's birthday party at her new place right on the beach in Malibu. Then Kiley had definitely gotten on the model's bad side when she'd joined a protest because Marym was not allowing the public access to the beach. Only it had turned out that since Marym had just purchased the house, she hadn't even known she was required to provide access via a path on her property. The protesters, including Kiley, had been both premature and wrong.

Even that wouldn't have been so bad if Kiley hadn't known that Marym had been involved with Tom before Kiley had met him. Kiley suspected that they'd had a torrid affair, and that Marym had an interest in picking up wherever it was that she and Tom had left off.

"Imagine running into you!" Marym exclaimed in husky, Israeli-accented English. She kissed Tom softly on the lips, then her gaze went to Kiley. "Oh. Hello, Kiley," she added coolly. "Nice to see you, too."

Tom put a protective arm around Kiley's shoulders. "We're celebrating," he explained. "Kiley thought she was going to have to go back to Wisconsin, but she just found out she's staying in L.A."

Marym smiled. "Great news. I'm happy for you."

Kiley tried to smile back, because Marym seemed to mean what she said. Kiley could never quite be sure if the problem between them actually existed, or if she was simply insecure and jealous around the gorgeous It Girl of the moment—the It Girl who knew Tom very, very well.

"Thanks," she replied. "I'm looking forward to it."

Marym tugged on Tom's hand. "There's no need for you two to wait. Come sit with us. We're in our booth in back with La Daga"—she put an ironic twist on the name—"and some other models, dishing about FAB. It was insane, wasn't it?"

Tom and Marym had both modeled in FAB and had shared a

table at the charity dinner aboard the *Queen Mary* ocean liner that had ended the FAB week festivities. That dinner had been organized by Esme's bosses, Diane in particular. After that dinner, Kiley reminded herself, Tom had come to find *her*. They'd kissed for the very first time on the deck of the vessel.

Take that, Marym, she said mentally, trying to buoy her self-confidence. *He could have stayed with you that night, but he came to me instead.*

She leaned in closer to Tom, sure that he'd politely turn down Marym's invitation to join the table of models. He'd tell Marym that he wanted to be alone with Kiley. It would be so wonderful and romantic and—

"Sure, we'd love to join you," Tom said easily. "Kiley?"

"Oh, yeah, sure!" she agreed, lying through her teeth.

Damn all over again. She couldn't very well say no, so she slapped a hap-hap-happy smile on her face as Tom and Marym led her to the back of the rowdy restaurant to join the beautiful people.

11

"So, bottom line, you need to learn how to drive," Billy concluded as he and Lydia walked hand in hand along the wet sand, stepping up the beach from time to time to avoid the incoming tide.

Billy had taken her to Mia-Mia's, a little Italian-themed coffeehouse in Redondo Beach, where they'd shared weak espressos and dry pastries while listening to a woman sing and play guitar on a small, raised stage in the corner. Lydia decided that her voice resembled a squealing squirrel monkey in heat, and her original songs all seemed to involve women deeply depressed over lost love.

Lydia sized up the situation thusly: the girl had been hired for her eye-popping cleavage, amply displayed in a silver brocade sweater unbuttoned to her navel, which was pierced with a diamond stick-pin, and for her legs, which were barely covered by a Seven for All Mankind denim miniskirt, below which she wore ripped thigh-high fishnet stockings and Balenciaga by Nicolas Ghesquière stiletto heels with black and silver velvet polka dots.

When she shared her observations with Billy, he pretty much agreed. The only reason he'd picked the spot was because as kids, he and X used to come to an Italian ice cream parlor that had been at the same address. It was the nostalgia factor that had seduced him into checking out the coffeehouse. Lydia found it sweet that a guy who had grown up in so many different countries—Mozambique, Germany, Thailand, Liberia, and, of course, the U.S.A.—could be so nostalgic about a simple neighborhood ice cream parlor.

The more she thought about it, though, the better she understood. She hadn't been back to Houston since she was eight years old, but there were places in her memory that still loomed large. Houston was home, and it would always be home, no matter where she lived in the world. As soon as she had the chance, as soon as she had enough money for a plane ticket, she planned to return to what she still thought of as *her* city, to revisit the glory days of her rich and pampered youth.

Mia-Mia's was only a block from the Pacific. By mutual decision, they left the coffeehouse halfway into the singer's first set. It was a glorious June night, and they decided to walk over to the beach. It was a wise decision. Whatever Mia-Mia's had lacked in inspiration, the ocean and the night sky made up for. On the walk over, Lydia told Billy the whole story of the moms' "X Is No Longer Your Driver" edict.

He whistled. As everyone knew, Los Angeles without wheels was not doable.

"So, two things. I need to learn to drive, and I need a car. I *need* a car."

Billy bent down and plucked up a seashell, then hurled it into the inky water. "I can't help you with the wheels, but I can teach you to drive."

"I'm not so sure that's a great idea," Lydia mused. "Maybe I should ask X for lessons. Havin' your boyfriend teach you to drive might be relationship suicide."

He put an arm around her slender waist and bumped his hip playfully into hers. "O ye of little faith."

"Oh, I have a whole lotta faith in all kinds of things," Lydia corrected. "Just to be on the safe side, though, maybe we should have sex before we start the driving lessons."

Billy threw his head back and laughed. "Come on, fess up. If I spent every waking hour trying to seduce you, you'd be telling me to back off."

She stopped walking, turned to him, and grabbed a handful of his navy blue T-shirt. "Totally wrong, Billy Martin." She stood on her tiptoes to kiss him softly. He kissed her back, and it quickly turned steamy. She felt his hand edge under the waistband of the extremely used but new to her vintage Missoni pink and black knit skirt she'd unearthed late that afternoon at Her Closet on Melrose, a hole-in-the-wall thrift store in Brentwood that was on the way home from the country club. When she'd tried on the size-six skirt, it had hung loosely on her hip bones (a six was way too big for her). Its hem grazed her knees, there was a cigarette burn on the right thigh, and the pink lining hung haphazardly from the bottom of the skirt—all of which accounted for its twelve-dollar price tag. Well, the low-slung waist worked in her favor, Lydia figured. And the price was right.

She'd brought it home and performed the same machete fashion surgery that she'd done on clothes in the Amazon, except this time with some pinking shears. Now the skirt fluttered midthigh. Then she'd dived into the bottom of her purse to find the engraved matches from the FAB party aboard the *Queen Mary*. She lit one and made a few more burn holes in the skirt's fabric to match the one that was already there, so that the burns looked punk and deliberate. She paired the skirt with a thin, cheap, boy's white sleeveless undershirt (thrift store price was a buck) and wore nothing underneath but creamy skin. No mention had been made of the "borrowed" cosmetics and perfume, so Lydia had been able to do her usual five coats of Benefit BADgal Lash mascara, several sweeps of Nars blush in Orgasm, plus a thick layer of collagen-infused lip-plumping gloss.

Evidently the entire effect had worked; she'd been gratified to see Billy's IQ drop when he picked her up and took in the hotness that was her . . . which made it all the more maddening that the boy refused to take her virginity.

She rubbed up against him, fingering the fly of his Levi's; she felt his hand caressing the minuscule Wendy Glez lace thong under her skirt. Oh yes, this was going very, very well. She tugged him down toward the sand. He obliged, kissing her neck. But then he whispered in her ear: "Not gonna happen here, Lydia."

Damn him.

She pushed against his chest. "If you really wanted me, you wouldn't have so much self-control."

He put his palms in the sand and leaned back, staring out at the ocean. "Look, you want this to be some quickie thing, I can oblige you. But I want more."

"Great idea! Quickie sex and then move on to something more?"

"It doesn't work that way. At least not for me." He scooped up a handful of sand and let it run through his fingers. "It's all fantasy to you, Lydia. But in my experience, sex too soon ruins a relationship."

She thought about that for a moment. "Is that because you're not very good in bed?"

He laughed. "Oh no, Miz Chandler. I'm not playing that game with you. Let's talk about driving."

Lydia pouted her incredibly pouty lips. "You are a very difficult person."

"So are you," he said, but he smiled when he said it, and gave her a kiss. "When do you get a day off? We'll do your first lesson."

She cocked her head at him. "You're sure?"

"My friend Sasha taught me on the Autobahn between Cologne and Bonn when I was fifteen," Billy explained. "It's not legal to drive in Germany until you're eighteen, but that doesn't seem to stop anyone. Speeds on the Autobahn run somewhere between eighty and time warp. I promise that you'll have an easier time of it than I did."

"Sold." Lydia lay back on her folded hands and stared up at the stars. "Great night, huh?"

"Oh yeah." Billy lay down next to her. "I used to look up at the stars when I was in whatever foreign country my parents had been transferred to and watch for meteors. I always wished to come back to America. You can't imagine how much time X and I spent on this beach, right here, when we were kids."

She turned to him, studying his profile in the moonlight. Chestnut brown hair flopped boyishly on his forehead. "I did that, too. Wish to come home, I mean."

He let his hand drift atop hers. "Yeah?"

"Yeah." She smiled at him. One of the big things they had in common was that neither of them had grown up in America. In his case, it was due to his parents' careers in the State Department as Foreign Service officers. Both of them knew what it felt like to know that America was home and to long to be there, but at the same time to feel like a stranger in your own country when you were back. It was like permanent culture shock.

She snaked her arms around his neck and kissed him. "I have Sunday off."

He kissed her back. "Excellent. I've got a thing at eleven, but after that."

Lydia couldn't help herself. "What thing?"

"A friend asked me to help out with a house she's building in Alhambra. It's part of Habitat for Humanity."

Lydia arched a brow.

"I have friends who are girls, Lydia," Billy said of her look.

"Me too, Billy. I'm not the jealous type. I was just wondering."

"Becca. She's another one of Eduardo's assistants."

Eduardo was the slave driver for whom Billy was interning in interior design. This Becca—whoever she was—must be an interior design student too.

"Have you had sex with Becca?"

Billy's eyebrows rose. "You really want to go there?"

"So you have?"

Billy sat up. "We met at Eduardo's Christmas party last year. She got wasted, I got wasted—"

"And you did it," Lydia filled in.

"Yeah, it happened," Billy admitted. "But we're just pals, Lydia."

"Friends with benefits," Lydia mused. She sat up too. "Are you *friends*?"

He ran a hand softly through Lydia's shagged silver-blond mane. "The only woman I want benefits with is you, Lydia. And for now, only in my dreams."

Ooh. There went that shivery feeling he gave her whenever he talked about her—them—and sex.

"Just remember, Billy," she whispered. "When we finally do jump each other, you're gonna have a whole lot of time to make up for."

He kissed the spot where her collarbones nearly met. "Count on it," he said.

The next thing she knew she was in his arms again. Then a bright light shone in their eyes, blinding them.

"What the—" Billy barked.

Lydia shielded her eyes from the light and looked up at a park ranger. He had a green uniform, a blond crew cut, and beefy arms, and he didn't look happy.

"This beach closes at ten p.m.," he roared.

"Yeah, we get that. Could you move the flashlight out of our eyes, please? It's a killer," Billy requested.

The park ranger stood his ground. "As soon as you two lovebirds move along and out of here."

Billy cursed softly under his breath and helped Lydia to her feet. "You seem way too happy in your work, man."

"Just move along," the ranger insisted, shining his light up the beach, presumably the path that he wanted Lydia and Billy to follow.

Lydia shook her head. "You know, there are other outlets

for your sexual inadequacies than bustin' up other people's romances."

"*What* did you say?" the ranger fumed, and made a motion toward his handcuffs.

"She's joking," Billy assured him quickly. "And we were just leaving. Come on, Lydia."

Billy took Lydia's hand and led her quickly through the sand until they reached the street.

"*Never* joke with anyone in a uniform in Los Angeles," Billy instructed. "They don't have a sense of humor."

"Who was joking?" Lydia asked. "I know sexual frustration when I see it. Or feel it."

Dang. She suspected she could have pushed Billy past the point of no return if the Sex Pistol hadn't shown up. Of all the rotten luck.

12

The Eurocopter AS 355 helicopter raced east, high above Jamaica's northern coastline. Esme pressed her face against the window, looking down at where the azure Caribbean Sea brushed the emerald island. The sky was cloudless, the horizon boundless. She thought she'd never seen anything as beautiful in her life.

"What do you think?" Steven Goldhagen, dressed in jeans and a promotional T-shirt from *Cedars of Hope,* one of his television shows, leaned toward her.

"It's amazing," Esme breathed.

"Not scared to be up here?" he asked.

Esme shook her head. "I think it's cool."

"*¡Mira, Esme, mira!*" Weston was pointing to the northern horizon. "*¡Yo puedo ver Cuba!*"

Esme laughed.

"What did she say?" Diane asked.

"She said she could see Cuba from up here," Esme reported.

Diane laughed. "Well, if we were higher, we probably could. Anyway, it's just another ten minutes or so, then we'll be back on the ground at the resort. Enjoy the view."

The view was remarkable, but no more so than the events of the past sixteen hours that had brought Esme to this place. When she'd come home from the country club, there'd been a limo waiting to take her to a passport-expediting agency. Esme didn't have a passport, and without one, she wouldn't be able to clear Jamaican immigration in Montego Bay. Within an hour, the photographs had been taken, the application had been made at the federal building near UCLA, and a new blue American passport had been in Esme's hands. After that, the limo had brought her back to the Goldhagens' estate, where she had packed not only for herself (in a piece of lime green Kate Spade luggage that Diane gave her), but also for the twins. They were only partially tracking what was happening; they knew they were going on a trip, but whether that trip was to Santa Barbara or Timbuktu didn't seem to be registering. Diane had left strict instructions about what they would need for five days in Jamaica—to Esme, it seemed like enough clothes and gear to last a month (six bathing suits, eight pairs of shorts, Wrist Wrapper watches custom-designed with actual diamonds, Minnetonka suede moccasins, and ribbed tank tops that blared ROCK STAR in rhinestones for each girl)—but she had dutifully followed the list.

It was two o'clock in the afternoon Jamaica time; the family had left the small Van Nuys airport on a private Gulfstream jet at eight o'clock in the morning, Los Angeles time. Steven had hastened to explain that the jet wasn't his—he considered anyone who actually owned a private jet to be wasting money that could be better donated to charity—but that he owned a share of it, which entitled him to five days of use in any given month.

On the plane itself, though, Esme had discovered a brochure from the company that operated the plane. The cheapest share that you could buy cost nearly four hundred thousand dollars a year, and that was for only fifty hours of flying time in the company's smallest jet, called a Hawk. This was not a Hawk, but a Gulfstream V that could carry eight passengers, plus a crew of four.

Esme had never been in a private jet before—she'd never even flown in an airplane. It made her giggle to think that the twin girls had more experience with flying than she did, having flown back to America from Colombia with Diane. The gleaming white plane was marvelously well appointed, with plush white Italian calfskin seats, a Denon sound system and Sony DVD player with a four-hundred-disc changer, a forty-five-inch flat-screen TV monitor, wireless Internet access, and a galley that had been stocked with bagels, lox, and Katie the pastry chef's special rugelach from Nate 'n' Al's delicatessen in Beverly Hills.

The pilot had told them that they could cruise at more than six hundred miles at fifty thousand feet, though he probably wouldn't be flying that high. Since the Gulfstream could fly from Saudi Arabia to New York without stopping to refuel, the relatively short hop from Los Angeles to Montego Bay, Jamaica, would be a breeze.

Commercial air travel time would have been five hours and forty minutes. The pilot assured them they could do it in four and a half. Not only could they, they would. He was absolutely true to his word. They touched down in Montego Bay four hours and twenty-nine minutes after they'd gotten airborne.

The helicopter buzzed eastward, with Easton and Weston

oohing and aahing at the sights, pointing down at the boats on the sea and over at the two-lane highway that hugged the coast. Esme could pick out the many resorts on the north coast—they were obvious from the hotel structures, swimming pools, golf courses, and immaculately manicured grounds. At times, they seemed to run right into one another.

The highway, though, also seemed like a line of demarcation. To the north of it were the resorts. To the south of it, the terrain and the architecture were starkly different. There were shanties and half-built structures; she even saw a dusty town with a public market swarming with shoppers. She couldn't tell exactly, but it seemed as though all the marketgoers were black.

Esme sighed. It never ended. No doubt everyone at the resort they were going to—she couldn't remember the name, but Diane had told her that it was the most exclusive one that permitted children—was going to be the same: richer-than-rich white people vacationing, poorer-than-poor dark people serving them, hoping for tips, eating their leftovers, et cetera et cetera.

God. She wasn't white, but she sure wasn't black. What would the help at the resort think of her?

That thought made her muse on what Jonathan would think. Would he even notice the disparity, or had he been so rich for so long that he'd just take it in stride that this was the way the world worked, that there would always be haves and have-nots? Jonathan was born a have, and Esme was born a have-not. That was just the way it was.

A short time later, the helicopter touched down on the helipad of the Northern Look resort, ten miles east of the Jamaican town of Ocho Rios. The helipad was painted blue, with a Jamaican flag in the center. As they had come down, Esme had seen a small army of white-jacketed Northern Look employees waiting for their arrival.

Now, as the chopper's blades stopped whirring, that army of employees was at their service.

"Welcome to Jamaica! May I take your bags, Mr. Goldhagen?"

"Welcome to Jamaica! May I bring you some champagne, Mrs. Goldhagen?"

"Welcome to Jamaica! May I show your family to its dwelling, Mrs. Goldhagen?"

"Welcome to Jamaica! May I reserve a tee time on the golf course for you, Mr. Goldhagen?"

It seemed to take only a few seconds for Steven and Diane to be loaded onto one green and white golf cart, with Esme and the twins on another one. A third golf cart, modified specially for the job, carried their luggage. Each cart was being driven by a handsome Jamaican guy—Esme found herself on the front seat of her cart, with the twins in the back. Her driver—a smiling fellow whose name tag announced that he was Desmond—kept up a running commentary as the golf cart wended its way toward the oceanfront. Esme found herself charmed by his singsong accent.

"On your left, you will find the golf course. It is twenty-seven holes, designed by Pete Dye, and we send out a foursome only every fifteen minutes so there is no waiting. On your right you'll find the children's circus section, with instructors from Moscow and Paris, an actual big top, and a flying trapeze. Straight ahead is our tennis center: four outdoor clay courts, two indoor hard courts. Our pros are members of the Jamaica Davis Cup team. I trust they will give you a game, yah mon," Desmond joshed.

The golf cart continued on the path, and Desmond continued

his narration. The resort was enormous. There was a yoga building, a health center, five restaurants—French, Japanese, Spanish tapas, Italian, and vegetarian—plus an outdoor buffet, a running track, a go-cart track, three swimming pools (one of them clothes optional), an enormous beach with every possible water sport from sailing to snorkeling to parasailing, and a main activities center in which Desmond promised they would find a small casino, game room, piano bar, and screening room. "Yah mon," Desmond reported. "You will not be bored here in Jamaica."

The one strange thing, though, was how few guests Esme noticed. There were several foursomes on the golf course, a group playing tennis doubles, and several others lounging around the main pool, which was teardrop-shaped and crystalline. But the whole Northern Look resort was amazingly uncrowded. She asked Desmond about that.

"Ah." He smiled as the golf cart neared a gleaming white modern structure by the beach. "We are very exclusive. Our clientele comes from all over the world—America, Canada, Argentina, France, Italy, even Taiwan. Yah mon. They are of . . . how do you say in America . . . a certain station. They do not want to be trampling each other."

"Oh," Esme said, wondering how much it cost a day to stay here.

Desmond smiled as if he was reading Esme's mind. "How exclusive are we? You do not stay in a room. You stay in a home. Each of these homes—where you will be staying—comes with its own chef, butler, and nanny for the children."

"Nannies for the children!" Esme exclaimed. "That's fantastic!"

Again, Desmond smiled. "I take it that you are the regular nanny to these children."

"I am their nanny, that's right."

The smile turned into a laugh, and Desmond stopped on the oceanfront side of the white building. It featured a beachfront patio with wicker furniture and a split-level layout with picture windows facing the ocean on both stories. There was an assortment of water sports equipment in a box on the patio—surfboards, masks and flippers, and a beach ball the colors of the Jamaican flag. Almost immediately, Easton and Weston hopped off the golf cart and charged over to the beach ball, which Weston kicked down the beach. The two girls ran after it, giggling with delight.

Esme felt like giggling, too. Five days down here without nanny duty? Where she'd just get to relax and enjoy herself, as if she was an actual part of the family? That was fantastic. In a way, it was better that Jonathan *wasn't* here. So much had happened these last few weeks, she could use some time to sort out her feelings about it all. . . .

The resort came with its own nannies. Right now, there was no place in the world that Esme would rather be than Northern Look.

As Desmond would say, "Yah mon."

"Esme, I'd like to introduce you to Peter and Erin Silverstein. Peter and Erin, this is our nanny, Esme Castaneda."

Esme marveled: Peter and Erin Silverstein were carbon copies of Steven and Diane Goldhagen, only five years younger. Just like Steven, Peter was a balding, fifty-something television producer with the deep tan of a several-times-a-week tennis player and the athletic build to match. Also like Steven, he had a scruffy, graying beard and was dressed in faded jeans and an orange tennis shirt. His wife, Erin, was a Diane Goldhagen clone, with a toned, tan body; surgeon-perfect nose and cheekbones; thick blond hair fortified with natural extensions; and a Pucci-print minidress.

"It's a pleasure to meet you, Esme," Peter said, extending his hand. Esme shook it.

"My pleasure," she told him, then shook Erin's hand too.

"So, you're the supernanny," Erin exclaimed. "Diane thinks you're God's gift to her children."

"Erin, don't say that," Diane mock-chided. "I'm going to have to give her a raise."

"How much are you paying her?" Erin shot back. "Because I'll double it. She can start tomorrow."

Steven laughed. "No chance. She's ours, now and forever."

Well, well, Esme thought. *Isn't this interesting. Forty-eight hours ago, I was afraid that Steven and Diane were going to fire me. Now I'm theirs, now and forever? All it takes is a little competition and a little interest from someone else, and they get all proprietary about me.*

"What are your girls doing?" Peter asked Steven.

"Sleeping," Esme interjected. "I think there's been too much excitement. Weston told me she wanted to go in the ocean, but she fell asleep putting on her bathing suit. Easton didn't even get that far."

"How about your kids, Erin?" Diane queried.

"We already dropped them at the kids' club up at the main building. Ham is playing with the Xbox 360, and Miles found someone to play Duelmasters with. He's kind of obsessed," Erin related. "I have to tell you, I'm looking forward to them joining up with your kids and—"

"Excuse me, guests."

They all turned—a tall, tuxedoed black gentleman with a mustache, carrying a tray, had just stepped into the expansive, white-on-white living room replete with wicker tables and squashy cream chaises. On that tray were four tall mimosas, two frozen brown and white cocktails, a sliced pineapple, a plate of sliced Gruyère cheese, and a sliced loaf of crusty French bread. This was the Goldhagens' butler, Samuel.

"Would Mr. Goldhagen and his guests like a snack before their afternoon activities?" Samuel queried.

"Just put it on the sideboard, Samuel," Steven suggested. "Or better yet, in the fridge. We're going to play some tennis, we'll attack it when we get back."

"Very good, sir," Samuel told them, in a more refined accent than Desmond's. "Have a good game. If you need new balls or anything else, we have a well-equipped pro shop."

"So, shall we?" Steven asked his friends. He held the door open. "We can get changed up at the clubhouse."

"Perfect," Erin said with a grin. "Esme, it was great meeting you. We'll see you for dinner."

"My pleasure." Esme flushed. She wasn't used to being treated with such respect.

After the couples departed, Esme found herself alone in the living room. It was blessedly quiet, save for the rolling in-and-out of the breakers. The windows had been partially opened—there was fine-mesh screening to keep out any insect life—and a breeze out of the north brought in not just the sound of the Caribbean Sea, but the smell of the salt air as well. It was absolutely intoxicating—more mind-altering than the drinks Samuel the butler had proffered.

Her home for the next several days wasn't bad, either. There were two different sleeping wings—one for the grown-ups, one for the kids. There were three spacious rooms in the kids' wing, all of them with oceanfront views, king-sized beds, TVs hooked up with PlayStations, and private bathrooms with shower, jetted tub, and bidet. As for the adult wing, Esme hadn't been invited down to take a look, but she could just imagine. The common areas included an eat-in kitchen (though Esme couldn't imagine why—who cooked when they went to a resort with five restaurants?), a playroom for the kids, and a fantastic living room, with its twin white love seats and big-screen Hitachi television. The living room also featured a full bar stocked with Bombay Blue Sapphire gin, Grey Goose vodka, and plenty of Jamaican Red Stripe beer, and a cabinet that held every game and puzzle known to mankind, an extensive DVD/CD collection, and a multilingual library.

The rug was handwoven Berber, and the art on the walls all Jamaican folk art. Esme had never been in as comfortable and welcoming a room in her life.

If only Mama and Papa could see this. They would love it. They work so hard, they deserve it as much as the Goldhagens do, and definitely more than I do. If only the three of us could be here together, for just one day—

Esme's reverie was interrupted by pounding on the front door of the house. "Hey!" a young voice was shouting. "Let us in!"

"Yeah, dude, let us in!"

Esme reached the front door a few moments after Samuel the butler, who'd already swung it open. Two scruffy-looking boys—approximately ages eight and six—came barreling through. One of them held a basketball in one hand and a football in the other, both of which he unceremoniously dumped on the floor at Esme's feet. The other boy turned to accost Samuel.

"Something to eat!" he bellowed. "We got something to eat?"

"Yeah," the younger boy chimed in, pushing past Esme into the living room. "We're hungry! Something to eat!"

As Samuel gave them a cockeyed look and then scurried away toward the kitchen, Esme frowned.

"Who are you boys?" she demanded.

"We're Ham and Miles!" the older one reported, at ear-splitting volume. "You're Esme, right? Our parents told us all about you! You're going to take care of us! Where's something to eat? I want something to eat!"

"No, I'm not." Esme was indignant. "There are nannies from the resort for that."

"No resort nanny!" the older boy shouted. His brother was already pawing through the DVDs. "We were at a resort with its own nannies before. Resort nannies are evil!"

"Yeah, listen to what Ham says," the smaller boy told Esme. At least he wasn't shouting. "Resort nannies suck!"

Maybe I thought too soon about the quiet. Anyway, just because—

"¡Hola, Esme! Hay demasiado ruido. Too much sound!" Weston stood in the entrance to the living room, rubbing her eyes. "Am tired. Want sleep."

"Me sleep too," added Easton, coming up behind her.

"Who are the girls?" Ham demanded. "I hate girls!"

"I hate girls too!" Miles said. "We're the He-Man Girl Haters Club! The only thing worse than resort nannies is girls!"

90

"*¿El no se gustan las chicas?*" Easton asked. "*¡El es un jopo!*"

"Easton!" Esme chided the girl automatically, trying to stifle a laugh. At the moment, she was in agreement. The boy *was* a *jopo*—an ass in Colombian Spanish slang.

"Something to eat!" Ham was shouting again. "Where's the food?"

Esme shook her head. Thank God there were nannies here, nannies that came along with the vacation whether Ham and Miles wanted them or not.

Of course, if there were nannies that came with the vacation, where were they? They ought to hurry up and arrive. The notion of being responsible for Ham and Miles Silverstein, in addition to the Goldhagen twins, was far too awful even to contemplate.

13

A black limo picked Kiley up at Jorge's house at eight-thirty in the morning. Before that, she'd profusely thanked her host for his kindness. His response had been bemused—if Kiley ever needed assistance, she should certainly count on him. Then he helped her load her bags, and she was on her way.

It took an hour and a half in the morning rush hour traffic to get to Evelyn Bowers's house on Rockingham in the tony Brentwood section of Los Angeles. Kiley had a tenth-grade teacher who had done a presentation on the O.J. Simpson murder trial of the early nineties, and she vaguely remembered that the former star football player had lived somewhere on this very street.

The Bowers home was exquisite from the outside. Two stories, with a white stucco exterior and brick front patio. There were two verdant orange trees whose leaves drooped over the patio; some of last season's oranges gave the air a pungent but pleasant aroma. Evelyn was not nearly as rich as Platinum, and you could definitely see neighbors' homes from the front of hers, but there was still no doubt from the locale that Evelyn was doing very nicely indeed.

The door swung open before Kiley could even press the doorbell.

"Welcome, Kiley, welcome!" Evelyn exclaimed. She was dressed casually, in jeans and a blue UCLA T-shirt, with Dansko Lana leather sandals on her feet. "Welcome to your new home! Let me help you with your things. No, drop everything inside, and I'll give you the tour. I can already tell this is going to be super."

Within seconds, Evelyn was leading Kiley through the interior of her impeccable home. The front hallway led into a sunken family room that had the biggest plasma television Kiley had ever seen, plus two southwestern-style couches and a Navajo rug on the floor. The artwork was also Native American themed, and ranged from sand paintings to feathered spears to actual Indian headdresses.

"Wow," Kiley breathed. She'd never seen anything like it. "Are you a collector?"

Evelyn shook her head. "Not really, but my ex-husband was. I got this stuff in the divorce settlement and I won't sell it because I want him to have the pain of seeing it on my goddamn walls when he comes to get the children for his visitation. I'll tell you, it's worth waiting all week for that moment. Come on, I'll show you the rest of the place."

Kiley followed as Evelyn continued the tour. As unassuming as the front of the house was, the interior was quite innovative. The place was U-shaped, built around an interior open courtyard that had soaring palm trees and a comfortable sitting area with stone benches and a large stone grill. Beyond it in the back were a paddle tennis court and a constant-flow lap pool, which Evelyn told Kiley she was welcome to use whenever she wanted.

The far end of one leg of the U belonged to Kiley. She had a cozy bedroom decorated in a Hawaiian theme, her own bathroom, plus a tiny refrigerator, microwave, and table built for two.

"Be discreet with whom you bring here, Kiley," Evelyn admonished her. "And keep clear boundaries between your personal life and my time. But our bedrooms are clear around the other side of the place. So . . . well, you know what I mean."

Kiley did know what she meant. Honestly, it was a little embarrassing. She couldn't imagine her own mother ever talking to one of her friends like that.

The rest of the tour went quickly. There were four other bedrooms—one for Evelyn, one each for her two children, and one for guests. The kitchen was forest green and opened onto the living room at the far end. Each of the bedrooms had its own bathroom, plus there was a simple half bath off the family room.

"Downstairs is fully finished," Evelyn reported. "Moon spends a lot of time down there, it's like his fortress of solitude. So, that's it. Would you like to go to your room and get unpacked, or what? We can call your mother later, if you'd like."

"When do I get to meet the kids?" Kiley asked her.

Evelyn ignored her question. "How about driving? Do you drive a stick?"

"Umm . . . no."

"That's good. I hate them. You'll take the Pontiac Vibe." Evelyn dug into her pocketbook, extracted an envelope, and handed it to Kiley.

"What's that?"

"Your pay," Evelyn announced. "A check for six fifty, as we discussed at the club. Dated for Friday. You can either deposit it or I'll cash it for you."

"You didn't have to do—"

Her boss smiled. "I wanted us to get off to the best possible start. The kids will be here soon, and then we won't have as much chance to—"

A car beeped three times in the driveway. "Ah!" Evelyn exclaimed. "They're here!"

She went to the front door and opened it; Kiley saw two children burst out of the backseat of a white Mercedes and come running toward them. Meanwhile, an older woman—a carbon copy of Evelyn except with thirty years on her (or it would have been thirty years, except for outstanding plastic surgery)—got out of the driver's side of the car.

"Get ready," Evelyn advised. "You're going to meet my kids and my mother."

Kiley got ready. But instead of stopping to say hello to their new nanny, the children ran right by her toward the house. There were a girl and a boy. Lydia had spoken to Kiley by phone and told her what she knew about the kids. They were Kiley's only reservation about taking this gig.

"We're going swimming!" the girl announced. She had curly dark hair and a sturdy figure.

"Swimming," the boy echoed. He was exceptionally thin, with an exceptionally long neck, and was obviously the younger of the kids. Then the two of them disappeared into their wing of the house.

"It's fine," Evelyn assured Kiley. "They're both excellent swimmers." She put her arms out to the older woman, who was now approaching her and Kiley. "Mom, hello. I want you to meet our new nanny, Kiley McClain. Kiley McClain, meet Carole-Ann Wolfenbarger."

Evelyn and her mother hugged while Kiley quickly decided not to correct her last name in front of Evelyn's mom.

"Please call me Carole-Ann," Evelyn's mom instructed. "I also answer to C.A. God, what a morning. Up at six for zazen, AA meeting at seven-thirty, pick up the kids at eight-thirty for art class . . . I'm already exhausted. Do you have any iced tea, Evelyn?"

"In the fridge, Mom," Evelyn said. "Kiley, will you excuse us for a few minutes?"

"Sure," Kiley told them. "I'll unpack and then keep an eye on the kids, okay?"

"Okay. Star and Moon will introduce themselves to you. They always do," Evelyn told her, then headed off with her mother. "If you get hungry, just come on to the kitchen. We've got a lot of everything."

Well, Kiley thought. *Not a bad start.*

As she started back to her bedroom, she mentally reviewed what Lydia had told her about Evelyn's children. Star was ten years old, in fifth grade, interested in ballet and singing, and by all reports reasonably normal. Moon, on the other hand, was supposed to be a lot more challenging. He was seven years old and suffered from a litany of alphabet disorders, including ADP (Auditory Processing Disorder), ADHD (Attention Deficit/Hyperactivity Disorder), and ABD (Antisocial Behavior Disorder) . . . at least according to his mother.

Kiley had mentioned this in her interview at the country club, but Evelyn had been extremely positive, after taking a few more verbal shots at Kiley's "friend-who-shall-go-nameless." Moon was on a BIP (Behavior Intervention Plan) and was under the care of the best child psychiatrists and neurologists at UCLA. He was monitored twice weekly in the office and once in the home. Kiley would have more support than she'd ever want.

That was good enough for her. She needed this job, big-time. Whatever the Bowers kids threw at her, she'd find a way to deal with it. She had dealt with her mother and father for seventeen years, which meant she had an awful lot of experience to fall back on.

She finished her long walk down the hallway and opened the door to her room. Then she gasped.

The room looked as if a tornado had blown through it. The bed was wrecked, clothes were strewn on the floor, and toilet paper was draped from the top of one window to the dresser and nightstands. The Bose Wave radio was blaring the news in some obscure Asian language, the water in the shower was running at the highest possible heat, and an unpleasant and thoroughly scatological odor emanated from the trash can near the desk.

"Crap," Kiley said aloud. "Thanks, guys. Nice welcome to the family. Really, really nice."

14

After three full days, Esme could have filed a very specific report on what was good about Northern Look: The food was amazing, beyond abundant, and available twenty-four hours a day. The grounds were lushly wild with thick hibiscus bushes and fragrant papaya and banana trees. Esme had taken several long walks along the fine sand on the beach and circumnavigated the premises a couple of times.

There was a walk-in aviary at the southeast corner of the property with several woven hammocks hidden among the palm trees, and that very morning—the kids were out on a glass-bottom boat voyage with their parents—Esme had impetuously borrowed a sketch pad and colored pencils from the arts and crafts center, settled into one of the secluded hammocks, and sketched several of the vivid green black-billed parrots that swooped through the guango tree branches. It was the first time in a long time that she'd been inspired to draw something other than tattoos, and it felt absolutely wonderful.

The Northern Look resort staff was extraordinarily professional, anticipating the needs of the clientele even before their customers thought of it. Guests who ventured into the ocean found not only thick, nine-hundred-thread-count sky blue towels waiting for them on their beach chairs, but also luxuriously fleecy terry cloth robes in the same color.

If they got hungry and didn't feel like venturing up to the restaurants, there were two snack huts at either end of the five hundred yards of private beach. One of them specialized in continental fare that could be grilled on the spot, like lamb chops and sirloin kebabs threaded with sizzling meats and verdant veggies; the other one was a genuine Jamaican jerk chicken pit that served the most succulent and spicy chicken Esme had ever tasted, along with a seemingly endless supply of Red Stripe beer. At both huts, you ate not on plastic beach tables, but on wrought-iron-and-glass tables covered with white tablecloths, and the finest Wedgwood china.

The resort's entertainment was outstanding. A house reggae band played at lunch and dinner, and there was always an after-dinner show. That night, illusionist Criss Angel was to dazzle the crowd by setting himself on fire and then disappearing. The night before, Sting, who was vacationing at Northern Look with his family, had strapped on a guitar and entertained the crowd with an impromptu acoustic set.

The legendary rocker wasn't the only celebrity at the resort. Esme recognized the senior senator from the state of California, the largest shareholder in a company that dominated the software industry (with his wife and children), and the host of a very popular television reality show that involved out-surviving the other contestants on some remote, rat-infested island or another.

There was more. Samuel the butler made sure that all the dirty capri pants, sandy Rosa Chá bikinis, and sweat-stained cargo shorts were washed overnight and delivered in a tissue-paper bundle on the home's front steps the next morning. She didn't have to fight to get the twins to sleep, since they were so tired by the day's activities that they drifted right off. She didn't even have to worry about Jonathan and Junior, because they were 2,500 miles away.

Her time at Northern Look should have been a real vacation—the operative word being "should." Only two things stood between Esme and semiparadise, and they were named Miles and Ham Silverstein. The boys had been right; their parents had zero interest in availing themselves of the services of the resort nannies, whom they didn't know, didn't trust, and pronounced "foreign." Esme found that last comment deeply ironic, because in fact, *they* were the foreigners.

Instead, the Silversteins expected that Esme would take care of their boys while they were off doing whatever they felt like doing. The Goldhagens tacitly acceded to this expectation. After the difficulties that she'd had with Diane just before they'd come to Jamaica, Esme didn't feel as though she was in a position to protest.

Ham and Miles were never still, and they pronounced every-thing at an ear-pounding volume—Esme couldn't imagine why. What was worse was that the twins had overcome their initial feelings and glommed on to the Silverstein boys as if they were junior role models. Whatever the boys wanted to do, the girls now wanted to do. Ham and Miles turned out to be the worst kind of influence.

Just outside the main breakfast buffet area—a magnificent open-air pavilion that faced the azure sea—the staff of Northern Look would post on a blackboard that day's planned activities, for both the adults and the kids. Listed at 10:30 a.m. was "Kids' Wacked-Up Relay." Esme had no idea what that meant, but when Ham and Miles got back from the boat ride they decided it would be their morning's prime activity—in the same shouted voices they always seemed to use. Esme was trapped. "Wacked-Up Relay" it would be, come hell or high water.

Now she stood near the shallow children's pool (which featured a mini pirate ship, complete with spraying water cannons) in a knot with seven or eight of the resort nannies, all of them young Jamaican women with accents so melodiously thick Esme could barely understand what they were saying. Meanwhile, the kids' activity director, a tall, chocolate-skinned, dreadlocked guy named Winston, was explaining the rules of the relay to the dozen or so kids between the ages of six and fourteen who were going to participate.

"Yah mon. This is how we do the wacky, wacky, wacked-up relay!" Winston announced, using a megaphone to amplify his words. Esme noticed that his muscles rippled nicely underneath his ensemble of white tennis shorts and creamy polo emblazoned with the navy Northern Look logo. "We have eight events you will have to do, visitors to Northern Look. First, I will throw coins to the bottom of the pool, and all of you must gather at least three. You do this one at a time. Then you run to the soda-bottle filling station and fill a soda bottle with a teaspoon. No Red Stripe bottles here! Then there's the you-and-your-nanny sack race, the you-and-your-nanny three-legged race, the you-and-your-nanny egg toss, and then finally, the last three events, which are a surprise until you begin them."

The local nannies smiled and nodded at their charges; evidently the relay was routine for them. It made sense—they worked here full-time. But for Esme, the idea of participating in a sack race, egg toss, or anything else with the human hurricanes, Ham and Miles, was not exactly appealing.

"What are the last three events?" Ham bellowed. "I wanna know!"

"Yeah, what?" Miles added.

"Yeah, what?" Weston echoed, her eyes shining in Miles's direction.

Winston smiled, his pearly teeth gleaming in the island sun. "You'll just have to see."

"I wanna know now!" Ham shouted, jumping up and down. "Esme, tell him to tell me now! Tell him to tell me!"

"Me too! Me too!" Weston and Easton screamed, stamping their magenta D&G sequined sneakers.

"You two need to behave," she told them in Spanish. "Don't copy these rude boys."

Suddenly, Ham, a whirl of blue jeans and a Dodgers baseball jersey, was at her side. "What did you say to them?" he demanded.

"I told them they needed to behave and that they shouldn't copy you and your brother when you are rude," Esme spit, even though she knew that it was an emotional response.

Miles's eyes grew wide. "I'm telling my parents what you said."

Go ahead, you little brat, Esme thought.

"I don't even want to play this stupid race, I quit!" Ham yelled.

"Yeah, me too!" Miles joined.

The twins immediately began screaming: "Me too! Me too!"

"If you would stop yelling we can continue with the fun," Winston explained in his musical lilt, keeping a pleasant smile on his face.

"So, who cares?" Ham yelled. "I think us kids should get to do what we want to do. Who wants to do cannonballs?"

Winston and the rest of the nannies were helpless to stop what happened next. Ham took a running start and did a monster cannonball jump into the children's pool. So did Miles, drenching his Kitson army fatigue shorts. After that, there was a virtual stampede to the children's pool, with each of the kids assembled for the relay doing a variation on a cannonball. Water splashed everywhere. Winston shrilly blew again and again on a silvered whistle that hung around his neck, but to no avail. Children were climbing out of the pool to cannonball again; Esme was glad that the pool was deep enough to handle their jumps, and was especially grateful for the swimming lessons that the twins had taken at the country club. Still, the other nannies and Winston were glaring at her as if *she* was the reason the planned activity had devolved to chaos.

"Those boys aren't even my kids!" Esme exclaimed. "I take care of the two girls!"

Winston shook his head and looked at the other nannies. "Dey not belongin' to any of us, girl," he said sourly, allowing his Jamaican patois to color his speech when the kids weren't listening.

Esme couldn't believe that this guy was dumping all the responsibility on her. She hadn't even met Miles and Ham until yesterday. "Don't blame me. Talk to their parents."

"You wanna get us fired from here, girl?" another nanny asked. "What if the boss man come along?"

"N-no, no, of c-course not," Esme stammered.

"Den I'm trustin' you ta find a way to control de boys." Winston shot an evil look at the pool, where Ham and Miles were engaged in an intense water fight aboard the pirate ship. In a fit of inspiration, Ham abandoned his post on the ship's deck, splashed back into the water, and began dunking one of the other boys. This started a dunking contest that the lifeguards had to break up with shrill whistles and threats to close the pool.

Esme strode to the water's edge. "Miles! Ham!" she yelled. "Get back here this instant. Weston and Easton, *vosotros también*!"

But Ham and Miles, in their matching soaked and squishing Nikes, ignored her completely and jumped back into the pool. The girls looked at them, looked at each other, and then followed the boys' lead.

"This is the worst day of my life!" Martina moaned, burying her face against Lydia's shoulder.

"I understand, sweet pea," Lydia told her, as soothingly as she could. "Just try to get through it as best you can."

"I liked things better before."

Lydia bit her lower lip in frustration. "Me too, sweetie. Me too."

Martina was right. It was only eleven o'clock in the morning, and it was the worst day of her life.

The day had started earlier than usual, with a five-thirty wake-up call for Lydia from Anya. Once again, Anya was the only mom in the house, since Kat had returned to New York for more tennis preparation. Anya had been curt on the phone. Skipping any niceties, she said that there was the usual list on the kitchen table of activities for the children, that she was going over to the Beverly Hills Hotel to hit some balls with some legendary Russian ballet dancer, and that she would be home for lunch. At lunchtime, she would question Jimmy and Martina about what they'd done that morning. If there was any deviation from the schedule at all . . .

Anya didn't finish that sentence, but Lydia knew exactly what she meant. She would have to play it by the book. Anya's no-nonsense, life-stifling book.

"Just two more sets," Lydia pleaded. "Then we can go home."

"I can't do any more sets," Martina moaned. "My legs hurt."

"Okay, well, a little break won't hurt. Then do one more."

Martina shook her head. "I can't even do one!"

The two of them were at the football stadium at Beverly Hills High School, on a day that was bright, cloudless, and very hot. The temperature when they'd left the house was 85° F, and the *Los Angeles Times* had warned of possible record-breaking heat that afternoon.

Notwithstanding the scorching weather, Anya's list for the day had been very specific:

TODAY'S SCHEDULE FOR MARTINA AND JIMMY

(Lydia—do not adjust schedule. Do not talk to me about adjusting schedule.)

6:00—Wake children. Shower. Dress. Apply SPF 30 sunblock to all exposed skin. Hydrate children with first 12-oz. bottle of water because of hot weather.

6:15—Swim. One quarter-mile for each child. No floats unless needed.

7:00—Breakfast. Soy granola, banana for Jimmy, blueberries for Martina, soy milk. Additional hydration of 12 oz. water.

7:30—Children to listen to Russian radio news broadcast on shortwave in my office. Just turn radio on, station is set.

8:30—Computer training. Jimmy has math and science. Martina literature and social skills.

10:30—Jimmy: tennis lesson with Oksana. Martina: physical training with you. You should bicycle with Martina down to the Beverly Hills High School football stadium, which is not being used because of summer. Bring plenty of Evian water. Dress Martina in a purple Nike Dri-Fit T-shirt, biking shorts, and trainers. Time Martina in lap time trial with stopwatch. Record time in notebook. Supervise "stadium stomping." Stadium stomping is Martina start at the bottom of stadium and run up aisle to top. Then she jog over to the next aisle and come down. Up and down three times!

106

Lydia, just out of curiosity (and as an inducement to Martina), had tried a single set of stadium stomps. It had been brutal—halfway up, she felt as if her legs wanted to jellify and stop working, and she knew that she was in a lot better shape than Martina, since she'd had no BMW with a driver in the Amazon. If her own muscled legs were hurting from the stadium steps, then what about Martina's?

Yet she couldn't let the girl just quit. For all she knew, Anya was sitting in the parking lot with a high-powered telescope. Or maybe one of the seemingly innocent workers tending to the well-manicured football field grass was on the payroll of the expatriate Russian Secret Police.

Lydia understood what was going on: It shamed Anya that her daughter was two standard deviations fatter than the norm and had overdeveloped breasts, to boot. Lydia had the feeling that if Anya could genetically reengineer her daughter to meet some mythic standard of perfection, she would.

As for Kat, Lydia couldn't help thinking of her as a not-so-innocent bystander. Why didn't she put her foot down? Was she afraid that Anya would leave her? As far as Lydia could tell, Los Angeles was full of lipstick lesbians who'd be only too happy to take the place of the Merry Matron of Moscow.

There was no doubt in Lydia's mind that the weight-loss strategy for Martina would backfire. First of all, she'd seen the girl's insatiable attraction to Lindt chocolates when she could get her hands on them. Lydia had no doubt that the reason the kids adored sweets so much was because they weren't allowed to have them. Plus, the older Martina got, the more she was going to resent Anya's rigidity. It was a perfect scenario for rebellion-by-consumption. And frankly, Lydia would be right there cheering Martina on.

Martina fisted some sweat from her forehead. "What's Jimmy doing now?"

Lydia understood that this question was a way of delaying the inevitable climbing of the stadium steps. She obligingly took out her list. "According to today's scheduled insanity," Lydia pronounced solemnly, "Jimmy is supposed to dig five thousand holes on the beach in Santa Monica, each hole exactly six feet deep and five feet wide. When he completes that task in under an hour, he is to swim to San Diego and back, towing an aircraft carrier."

Despite her tiredness, and a T-shirt that was soaked in perspiration, Martina laughed. "That sounds about right. Even though I read that book last year."

"What book?" Lydia feigned ignorance. She'd read an article about the popular kids' book-turned-movie, *Holes,* in one of the air-dropped magazines she'd gotten in the rain forest. "The one about the boy who towed an aircraft carrier?"

Martina cracked up again. "You know what I mean."

"I do. Listen, I got an idea."

"That we go home?" Martina asked eagerly.

Lydia opened one of the water bottles in her backpack and took a long swallow. What she was about to offer was significant, and would be a pain in the ass. On the other hand, she'd started a relationship with this girl, and she wasn't about to let Anya the Anaconda ruin it.

"No. But how about if I become your workout partner? If Anya asks you to do sit-ups, I'll do sit-ups with you. If she asks you to run, I'll run. If she wants you to swim, I'll swim. It isn't going to be easy for you, but if I'm doing it with you it'll definitely be a lot easier. So, what do you say?"

Martina gazed at Lydia in awe. Then, Lydia saw two crystalline tears roll down her cheeks—the girl made no effort to wipe them away.

"Are you mad at me or glad at me?" Lydia asked.

"Glad," Martina whispered, and hugged Lydia hard.

"I'm glad, too," Lydia told her. "We're in it together."

"I'm so happy that you're our nanny," Martina told her. "And our cousin."

"Me too, sweet pea." This lovefest was not getting Martina any closer to finishing her mother's assignment, but for just a moment, Lydia didn't care. When she'd been in the Amazon, she'd thought about things like family birthdays and wedding celebrations. She'd missed having those things with a big extended family, which was impossible in Amazonia. Her parents had made an effort in the rain forest to do things like birthdays and Christmas; there had even been an attempt to celebrate Thanksgiving. But it was always just the three of them. She had been to traditional Ama weddings and birthdays, even celebrated her birthday with a bonfire and python meat with the tribe, but it was nothing like being with family of your own.

This moment, here with her cousin Martina, reminded her of that.

"Come on," she told Martina, and then pointed to the stadium stairs. "Someone once told me that even the longest journey starts with a single step."

15

"I feel really, really . . . white," Tom joked as he and Kiley found the only empty table at La Verdad coffeehouse, on Alvarado Street in Echo Park. Other than the two of them, the clientele was entirely Latino, as it had been that first morning that Kiley had eaten at Bettina's.

"That's how I felt when I first came to this neighborhood, too," Kiley told him, finding it strange to be in the position of reassuring a guy. "But the more time I spend here, the more I think it's safe, especially on this street. No one's going to bother us."

"Are we even going to be able to order?" Tom asked. "I don't speak Spanish."

"There's an Anglo waitress who speaks English. Don't worry."

"I'm in your capable hands, then." Tom glanced around. "How'd you get to be such an expert on Echo Park?"

"I lived here for twenty-four hours," Kiley reminded him. "I don't know if that makes me an expert, though."

It was the night after Kiley's first day on the job with Evelyn Bowers. During the afternoon, Kiley had gotten a phone call from Esme's friend Jorge. He had heard that Esme was out of town with her employers, but he was going to be performing that night at La Verdad, and he wondered whether Kiley would be able to come. Then he added that maybe Kiley would like to bring a friend, or a few friends. He had ulterior motives, he confessed.

Was he intimating that he liked Kiley? As in more than a friend? And if he was, how did she feel about that? It wasn't as though she and Tom had something official going on. In fact, more often than not, Kiley suspected that Tom still had something going on with Marym. Marym seemed to think so.

"What's the motive?" Kiley had asked.

"I get a percentage of the cover charge."

Kiley had laughed, covering her secret thoughts. She said she'd call her friend Tom—why she hadn't called him her boyfriend Tom, she didn't know—and maybe they'd come together. She'd done exactly that, and then called Lydia, too. Lydia claimed that she was in the midst of the worst day of her life and if La Verdad laced its coffee with tequila, she'd definitely be there, and bring Billy too. Kiley had to admit that she didn't know the ingredients in their coffee, but that it would probably be a really different evening. That was good enough for Lydia.

True to Kiley's word, there was an Anglo waitress. Tall and bone-thin in that "if I'm not ten pounds underweight I'll look like crap in front of the camera" way that Kiley had come to understand was a local norm for movie and TV actresses, she had very high cheekbones, full lips, and honey-colored eyes that matched her long, curly hair. She wore a pair of low-slung denim bell-bottoms and an eye-popping Apple Bottom yellow tank top. A La Verdad apron was loosely tied around her taut waist.

"Welcome to La Verdad," she said. "I'm Christine. Your first time here?"

"For both of us," Kiley answered. "This is my friend Tom, I'm Kiley. I'm a friend of Jorge Valdez."

Christine's eyes grew wide. "You know Jorge? He's like a god around this place." She kept her eyes on Tom. "Do I know you from somewhere?"

Tom shrugged. "An audition, maybe?"

"No. . . ." She tapped a finger against her pouty lips, contemplating. Then her eyes lit up. "I know. The billboard! On Sunset, right?"

"Yeah," Tom admitted.

"Nice work," she complimented him, giving him a dazzling smile.

Work? Kiley thought. *What work? He just lay there in his boxers with a sexy look on his face.*

"So, what can I get you, Tom?" the waitress asked breathlessly.

"*I'd* like some *horchata*," Kiley put in before Tom could answer. Tom ordered coffee.

Christine motioned to the empty seats at the table. "Friends joining you?"

Kiley nodded.

"Other models?" she asked Tom.

Oh, for God's sake, this was ridiculous. "Could you just bring some water for all of us, please?" Kiley asked.

Christine's eyes slid to her. "Fine," she said coldly. "Jorge should be in to start his set in about a half hour." She headed off to the kitchen.

Rather than look at Tom, Kiley looked around until she cooled off. The waitress was so rude! Her Tom might as well be Tom Cruise, for the way the waitress had treated her.

Unlike Starbucks, there was no open coffee counter with a hip-looking barista mixing the mochaccinos. On the other hand, La Verdad was spiritually about as far from a Starbucks as could be. La Verdad was one of a kind. Starbucks was essentially apolitical, though it had a mildly pro-environmental, liberal bent. La Verdad was radical. *Way* radical. There were posters of Che Guevara, Cesar Chavez, and Fidel Castro, along with angry slogans written right on the brick walls in scrawled white paint. Kiley wished she could read Spanish: *"¡El pueblo, unido, jamás será vencido!"* Another one she could figure out: *"¡El socialismo ahora, el socialismo por siempre!"* There were picket signs from various demonstrations, posters from past performances at this very spot, and flags of many countries that she could only assume were Spanish speaking.

"Hey." Tom reached over and took Kiley's hand. "She got to you, huh?"

Kiley sighed. "Now I know how Katie Holmes must feel."

Tom laughed. "Hardly. I just ignore that stuff."

Kiley nodded, but she still felt irritable. Why hadn't Tom taken her hand while Christine was ogling him?

"We're not in the Midwest anymore, are we?" Tom asked, with a darling half smile on his face.

"No," Kiley agreed. "We're not." She returned his smile. Probably she was just overreacting, mostly because whenever she was with Tom, it brought out all her insecurities. On a hot-

or-not scale, Tom was beyond a ten. And Kiley figured that she was *maybe* a six or seven on a good day.

Her eyes slid over to him. Even now, when he was just wearing Calvin Klein jeans and a green T-shirt from Urban Outfitters (which wasn't too far afield from what most of the other customers had on), he was smoldering. As for Kiley, she was in her usual no-name jeans, a paper-thin gray hoodie, and black Cons.

"There's so much about the world that I still have to learn," Kiley found herself admitting.

"That's why you want to stay in California," Tom reminded her, still holding her hand. "So tell me, how's your new gig going?"

Kiley rolled her eyes. "You can't even imagine how nuts her kids— Hey, there's Lydia and Billy!"

She spotted her friends by the front door of La Verdad as they looked around uncertainly. Well, Billy did. Lydia had her usual insouciant smile as she got a look at the unusual surroundings. She was wearing a cleverly slashed Pucci dress dotted with psychedelic black and violet paisley, and slightly battered black lace-up sandals. Somehow she had managed to find designer clothes at a reasonable price and look completely unpretentiously sexy. Billy, meanwhile, was wearing an outfit similar to Tom's: jeans and a white V-neck T-shirt. Kiley waved. When Lydia saw her, she looped her arm though Billy's and led him over to the table.

"Everyone's met everyone at FAB, right?" Lydia asked.

Billy and Tom shook hands. "I understand you did some of the designing for the fashion shows," Tom said. "You're a very talented guy."

"I'm the low man on the totem pole; just followed orders,

but thanks." Billy helped Lydia into her seat, then pulled out a mismatched chair of his own.

"Now, see, he's way too modest," Lydia insisted. "Some of the best ideas were his, even if he didn't get credit." She glanced around at the heavily graffitied walls. "This is so much classier than an Ama fertility rite."

Their waitress, Christine, wound her way back to their table and set down Kiley's *horchata,* then gave Tom his coffee with, Kiley noted, a dazzling smile that had been recently amplified with coats of shimmering lip gloss. She sighed.

After Christine took Lydia and Billy's order, Lydia spun her orange plastic chair around toward Kiley.

"So, what's it like to work for Psycho Bowers?" Lydia demanded. "Is her family as nuts as she is?"

"You cannot even imagine," Kiley said, raising her voice over the increasing din in the coffeehouse. It was filling rapidly with buzzing patrons. Evidently the Latin Kings were a popular attraction in the neighborhood.

"Tell me everything," Lydia urged. "It has to be better than my gulag."

Kiley didn't even know where to begin. First there was the shock of returning to her room to find that it been trashed like an unpopular kid's house on Devil's Night. After she'd cleaned up her room had come shock number two. Evelyn's warm welcome had been a complete smoke screen. Not only did she expect Kiley to be the nanny, she also expected her to be her personal assistant. While grandma smoked and played gin rummy with her grandchildren, Evelyn put Kiley to work filing press releases and typing memos that Evelyn dictated at breakneck speed into a minicassette recorder.

"She loves the cassette recorder," Kiley reported. "She barely even speaks to me. She doesn't even leave notes. Instead, she leaves cassettes for me in a box outside her office."

"What about the kids?" Billy asked.

"What kids?" Kiley shot back. "They won't even speak to me! At least with Serenity and Sid over at Platinum's, I had a *relationship.*"

"Come on. They must have said *something* to you," Tom prompted, then edged his chair closer to the wall to accommodate a Latino couple—he with heavily tattooed arms, she with the tightest jeans on the largest butt that Kiley had ever seen—who couldn't find a seat but still wanted to see the show.

"Okay, well, let's see," Kiley mused. "I asked them who trashed my room, and they had absolutely no idea, maybe I was crazy and had done it myself because of the voices in my head. Oh, and they'd have to discuss my mental problems with their mom."

Lydia laughed. "Sorry. I mean, it sounds awful. But you have to admit, they're funny."

"Not so much if you lived it." Kiley shrugged. "It doesn't matter. I can put up with whatever. I need the job."

Christine squeezed through the crowd with Lydia and Billy's drinks, then took off again. A girl in high black stiletto-heeled boots bumped into Kiley's chair as she tried to get by.

"Who's playing here tonight? U2?" Tom quipped.

Lydia took a sip of her *horchata.* "Dee-lish," she pronounced, then put her elbow on the table and her chin on her closed fist. "So, Kiley, here's what I think. You ought to let yourself get poached."

"Poached as in . . . eggs?" Kiley ventured.

"Poached as in by another family. Blow this job off. Take another one."

"What other one?" Billy asked.

Lydia laughed. "Surely you jest."

"Isn't that . . . unethical?"

Lydia went wide-eyed. "Isn't it unethical for Evelyn to ask you to do her filing? Isn't it unethical that your boss wouldn't sit down with you and her kids and tell them who you are?"

"Well, yes," Kiley allowed. "But the way I see it, she's in the power position."

"And again I ask: what other job?" Billy repeated.

Lydia waved him off. "I'm getting to that." She leaned in toward Kiley. "Now, here's what I want you to do. If you wake up tomorrow and find yourself in Brentwood's version of hell, call me, and I'll take care of the rest."

Kiley raised a skeptical brow. "Lydia, no offense, but you couldn't even get your nanny business off the ground."

Again, Lydia waved a hand. "Do not clutter my head with past details," she decreed. "I have a brilliant plan that will—"

Suddenly, loud Latin music filled the air, drowning out the rest of Lydia's sentence. Kiley realized it would be futile to try to shout over it. She'd just have to wait to hear the rest of Lydia's "brilliant plan."

The lights in La Verdad dimmed; two spotlights illuminated the small stage, which featured a deejay booth and two standing microphones. The music lowered and an unseen announcer boomed out over the sound system: "¡Las señoras y los caballeros, residentes de nuestra aldea, es mi placer introducir a usted, Los Reyes Latinos d'Echo Park!"

The crowd applauded and whistled. It was so dense that

Kiley had to crane her neck to see the stage, where a trio of Latino guys, led by Jorge, bounded up onto the stage. They were dressed identically, in black jeans and black cotton long-sleeved shirts—a real departure from the hip-hop groups that Kiley was used to from MTV, where the rappers sported over-sized, diamond-dusted gold jewelry and bizarre, baggy, or just plain over-the-top outfits. This looked more as if Jorge and his friends were making a deliberate statement of group solidarity instead of personal stardom.

"Now, which one is Esme's friend?" Lydia asked over the crowd noise.

"In front," Kiley yelled back.

"Very tasty," Lydia opined, lightly licking her pouty lips.

Kiley found herself mentally agreeing with that assessment.

The deejay started scratching; Jorge and the other guy went to the mike.

> *"Una época vendrá, cuando se presentará el pueblo*
> *Una hora especial, un rato especial de la noche.*
> *Una época vendrá, cuando la gente estará libre.*
> *Una hora especial, un rato especial de la noche."*

"Anyone speak Spanish?" Lydia asked.

"A little," Billy said. "It's something like, 'A time will come, when the people will arise, a special time of day, a special time of night. A time will come, when the people will be free. A special time of day, a special time of night.' Or something like that."

"Wow," Kiley murmured, extremely impressed. She'd never been a fan of rap music; the macho-posturing, gay-bashing, and girl-demeaning lyrics made her sick to her stomach—that is, when she could understand the lyrics at all. But clearly the Latin Kings were different.

Jorge's rap continued, the deejay's scratching propelling the words along. The crowd started clapping their hands and whooping on the words *"libre"* and *"noche."* Then they started chanting along with Jorge.

Kiley couldn't help herself. She found herself chanting too, even though she had only the barest idea of what she was saying because of Billy's translation.

Suddenly, the rap stopped in the middle of a verse. At first, the crowd applauded and cheered, thinking that this was a deliberate artistic choice. Then there was booing, which grew louder and louder. Most of the patrons of La Verdad got to their feet, which blocked Kiley and her friends' view.

"What's going on?" Lydia demanded.

Billy climbed up onto his chair to try to get a better look. "It's three people in firefighters' uniforms. They're talking to Jorge and someone else. A really tall skinny guy with a mustache."

"He's the manager," Kiley reported, remembering her meeting the day before when Jorge had tried to get her the waitressing job.

"Must be overcrowded in here," Tom guessed. "Well, that's no shocker."

Two minutes later, after remonstrating unsuccessfully with the firemen, Jorge was back on the mike.

"I'm speaking in English so our friends the firefighters can understand me," Jorge announced. "We've got a problem here tonight. Too many of you wanted to come hear the Latin Kings!"

The crowd cheered.

"Problem is, capacity of La Verdad is seventy-seven, and we're way over," Jorge continued. "The law is gonna shut us down for tonight."

The crowd booed and pointed their thumbs downward.

Jorge motioned with his hand for them to quiet down. "But here's what me and the boys are gonna do. We'll play *two* shows tomorrow night, nine and eleven. We'll hand out passes on the way out. Come back with your passes," Jorge advised, "and you can come in for no cover. For right now, let's ease on out of here *sin problemas*. Okay?"

"Keep playing!" someone shouted from the back of La Verdad to thunderous applause. "What they gonna do, teargas us?"

"Know what?" Jorge asked rhetorically, gesturing toward the other guys on the stage. "Me and the boys, we're the first to go. Come on, *cholos*. We show some respect to our firefighters. Someday they may have to save your life." And with that, they marched off the stage and into the cheering crowd.

"He's leaving the stage," Billy reported. "He's out the door."

With Jorge and the Latin Kings gone, the crowd began to disperse. Tom insisted on picking up everyone's check, and soon Kiley and her friends were out the door too.

But an image of Jorge up onstage stayed in her mind. There was something so compelling about him. So . . . so admirable. And somehow—Kiley couldn't quite figure out why—it was damn sexy.

16

After the aborted outing to La Verdad, the group went to a diner in Silverlake that Billy had suggested called Millie's. He said it had been around forever. He was right; their waitress told them that the place first opened in 1926. Judging by her grizzled face and gruff voice, Kiley suspected that the waitress had been working there since the beginning.

The food was excellent, though. Kiley had ordered something called the Devil's Mess, which was scrambled eggs, turkey pieces, cheese, and spices, all topped by an enormous dollop of homemade salsa, plus guacamole and sour cream. Far too much food for Kiley to eat by herself, but luckily Lydia—who, despite her thin frame, had never met a plate of food she didn't like— finished it off, in addition to her cheeseburger deluxe with a double order of fries. Where the girl put it, Kiley had no idea. Evidently she was blessed with a fast metabolism, thanks to years of running around the Amazon jungles. Lydia claimed she was making up for all those years of eating monkey meat.

After dinner, they'd gone their separate ways. Billy and Lydia decided to go shake their tail feathers at LAX (the nightclub, not the airport); Tom and Kiley opted to take in the Alexander Payne film marathon at the Grove. When the back-to-back showings of *Election* and *Sideways* were over, Kiley expected that Tom would drive her back to Brentwood, back to Evelyn Bowers's house. She found herself dreading the thought. What would she find when she let herself back into her room? A living pile of hungry red ants? Essence of rotten eggs? Mud-covered livestock?

Just as she was contemplating this depressing scenario, she realized that instead of going west on Wilshire, Tom was driving north on La Brea.

"This isn't the way to Brentwood, is it?" Kiley asked.

Tom's eyes flicked to her, then back to the road. "I was thinking we could go to the Hotel Bel-Air."

That statement hung in the air between them. The Hotel Bel-Air was where Tom lived. Kiley knew that only too well, having briefly occupied the suite next door to his during the shooting of *Platinum Nanny*. In fact, that was how they'd met, after she'd heard him through the wall during the night, making what had sounded like insanely passionate love. The next morning, they'd walked out of their suites at the same moment. She'd been almost too embarrassed to make eye contact.

"Kiley?" Tom questioned.

"Yes? I mean, that's my name." She giggled at how ridiculous she sounded. "Okay, that was an idiotic thing to say. I'm just . . ." She could feel her cheeks burning.

"We can listen to music, watch TV, or . . . whatever," Tom explained. "It'll be your call. So . . . we good?"

"Good," Kiley managed to squeak, her lips suddenly feeling parched.

Tom nodded, turning onto Sunset Boulevard. "What time do you have to be up in the morning?"

"Nine," she squeaked again. Why was he asking her that if they were going to watch TV? Obviously they weren't going to watch TV *all night*. She would only still be there in the morning if . . . So that had to mean that he wanted to . . . maybe even *expected* to . . .

Oh God.

"Nine it is," Tom said easily.

They didn't talk the rest of the way back to the hotel. Tom popped a White Stripes CD into the player and music filled the air, covering the silence between them until Tom pulled into the hotel's roundabout.

It wasn't as if Tom had a roommate. It wasn't as if his parents or her parents could knock on the door and interrupt them. That saying, be careful what you wish for? Well, this was what Kiley had wished for. Now that the moment appeared to be at hand, all she felt was petrified.

She wasn't technically a virgin. At least she didn't *think* she was. There was that horrible night with her then-boyfriend, Stuart. Everything had happened so fast; she wasn't really sure what had happened at all. If he had or if he . . . hadn't. They had used a condom—Stuart had had one. It hadn't hurt. Right after it—whatever "it" was—Stuart had wanted to get up and go right back to the party at his next-door neighbor's house. That was the first and only time they'd done it, and they'd broken up shortly thereafter.

That couldn't have been sex, could it? It had been just so . . . so nothing. Maybe there was something wrong with her. Anatomically. Or emotionally. Or—

"Kiley?"

Tom and the parking valet both stood at her side of his truck. The door was open, meaning one of them had opened it, and she still sat in the cab.

Tom held out a soft hand. Kiley took it and allowed him to help her out.

"Sorry," she murmured. "Lost in thought."

"No problem."

Tom put a hand at the small of her back to guide her into the hotel. Kiley wondered if he could feel the pudginess protruding slightly out the top of her jeans, the jeans she had had so long, they were grayish instead of blue on the butt and knees. She was five foot six and a hundred and thirty-six pounds, which wasn't fat but was also a long, long way from Los Angeles norm, which was probably a good ten—no, *twenty*—pounds thinner. She sucked in her stomach as she preceded Tom past the hotel's luscious wooden entry and into the plush lobby. Its opulent creamy walls with golden and walnut finishes were matched only by the vibrant gardens that bloomed all year round.

Probably she looked reasonably skinny standing up. But what about sitting, when her body sank into the feather-soft furniture? Would her stomach pooch out? Would Tom touch it and be repulsed? Wasn't he used to skinny, perfect supermodels like Marym?

Tom guided her past another couple, she in a sleek black

cocktail dress held up by an art deco diamond brooch over one shoulder, he in a tuxedo. The woman looked utterly serene, with a swanlike neck and mile-long legs that ended in black satin open-toed Jimmy Choo pumps. Sure, she could look serene. She probably looked like a goddess naked. Whereas Kiley—

And then it hit her. What if Tom wanted to have sex *with the lights on*? He'd be able to see every imperfect pudge on her body. He'd see her remove her cheap cotton Kmart undies. Or maybe he'd want to remove her cheap cotton Kmart undies. How embarrassing would *that* be?

Stop it, she told herself. *Stop it right this damn second. Tom Chappelle could be with a million girls. He's here with you because he wants to be with you. And you want to be with him.*

"After you," Tom offered, after he slid his key card into the door's security slot and held the door open for Kiley.

"Thanks." She walked past him and entered his suite.

Kiley had been in the suite before; she'd gone there the night Platinum had been arrested. But of course, that visit had not been about sex. It looked exactly the same: white Italian couches in the living room with a glass-and-gunmetal coffee table. Persian rugs on the floor, twentieth-century art on the walls, big-screen TV with DVD system. Kiley remembered that there were two bedrooms, plus a full kitchen with Swedish modern appliances. When she'd been here before, there had been a fresh fruit basket on the kitchen table. Now, there was an extravagant tiger lily floral arrangement on a side table in the living room.

But this time, she wasn't too distraught over the trauma of

the evening's events to think about the lust symphony she'd heard coming from this very suite: moaning, screaming, bed-bouncing, window-rattling, wall-shaking sex. Kiley remembered lying there, and what she had been thinking about. First, she had sincerely hoped that her mother couldn't hear what she was hearing. Second, she had sincerely hoped that the erotic variations on a theme in ecstasy would come to a mercifully rapid conclusion. Last, when the serenade went on, and on, and on, she had thought that whoever was in that room was having a hell of a better time than she had experienced with Stuart. Also: *One day, I hope that's me.*

Well, maybe this was the day. Night. Whatever.

"Are you okay?" Tom asked her. They were in his living room now.

"Fine, sure, just super!" Kiley chirped.

Tom frowned. "Your cheeks are all red. Do you feel okay?"

Oh crap. Why did she have to blush like the almost-redhead she was? "No, no, I'm fine. How about a drink?" Kiley asked boldly. There. That had sounded normal. She hoped.

Tom grinned. "The girl who doesn't drink asks for a drink?"

Oh crap again. He remembered that she didn't drink. "I'm full of surprises," she uttered, trying to sound mysterious. All she sounded, however, was insipid, at least to her own ears.

Tom moved to the suite's bar, which was stocked with top-shelf liquor: Stoli vodka, Maker's Mark bourbon, rum from some obscure Jamaican distillery, and the like.

"Vodka tonic?" Tom asked. "And sit down, please, you're making me nervous standing there in the middle of the living room."

Flustered, Kiley sat down on the couch and looked for something to do with her hands. There was a copy of *Los Angeles* magazine on the coffee table between the couch and the love seat, so she picked it up and started to leaf through it. Then she remembered that Tom had asked her about a drink, and stood expectantly at the bar.

"A vodka tonic would be fine," she told him, though she'd never had one in her life. "Tonic" made her think of hair tonic, some ancient chemical concoction her grandfather used to use on his hair. The last thing she could remember drinking was champagne with Esme and Lydia, a couple of weeks before. Her father's affinity for the product of the brewery where he worked made her very, very leery of alcohol. Yet, nervous as she was to be alone with Tom in his suite, a drink seemed like the thing to do. When Tom brought her the highball glass—he'd made one for himself as well—she drained a quarter of it in one slug.

"Easy there, girl," he cautioned.

"I'm fine," she told him breezily, as if she threw back vodka tonics every day.

"I'd have to agree. Say, hold on a sec. I want to show you something."

Without waiting for her answer, he bounded up and went into his bedroom. It made her nervous all over again. What was he doing? Would he come back in a robe? Was he in there lighting candles and putting on mood music? Would they end up on the same bed where he and whoever-it-was-who-was-having-a-terrific-time had made beautiful music together? Would he—

Oh God. What if he came back naked?

Please-please-please don't let him come back in here naked.

She took another huge gulp of her drink and stared at the blank big-screen TV.

I don't know if I'm ready for this.

"Hey," Tom said softly. "Look at this."

Kiley turned, half-shutting her eyes. Whew. He was fully dressed, a leather-bound album under his arm.

"Photos," he explained, almost shyly. "From Iowa. Me and my family, me growing up. I was thinking that you might want to see them." He scratched his clean-shaven chin. "There really isn't anyone else here in L.A. who has any interest in—"

"I'd love to see them," Kiley said; it was the first honest thing she'd uttered since he'd informed her they were heading to his hotel. He really wasn't so different from her, she reminded herself. Until just a few months ago he'd been living on his parents' farm.

He grinned and sat next to her. "Well, all right, then."

For the next fifteen minutes or so, Kiley looked through Tom's photos. His enthusiasm and nostalgia for home was heartwarming to her, even if she didn't share the sentiment about La Crosse. Tom clearly loved and missed his big, rambunctious, incredibly photogenic family. Kiley missed her mom sometimes, and her best friend, Nina. Sometimes she wished she could sleep in her own bed. But other than that . . . no. Few things made her happier than being out of La Crosse, Wisconsin.

Tom closed the photo album. "So, that's me."

"If you weren't so handsome, you'd be normal," Kiley kidded. She was pleased that she could even make such a joke. Maybe it meant that she actually was relaxing. Relaxing would be good. Plus, she felt warmer, but in a good way. That had to be from the drink. It tasted bitter and vile, though.

"I'm just a farm boy from Iowa who stinks of shit in the

spring." He casually draped an arm around her shoulder. "Cow shit, that is."

Kiley laughed and let herself melt against his body. "My grandma used to call that the smell of money." He kissed the top of her head. "But maybe I should ask you to take a shower."

Kiley was shocked by her own words. Had she really just said that? It sounded so flirtatious, so seductive, so—

"How about if we take one together?" he suggested. His voice sounded thick with desire.

Holy shit. Red alert! Red alert! Kiley sat up and drained her drink. "Um" was all she could think of to say.

"Kiley." Tom pulled her close and gently kissed her. It was wonderful. The kisses continued, becoming more passionate. Who had invented making out? That person was a genius.

"Shower?" he murmured into the nape of her neck.

"I—I—" she stammered. Then he was kissing her again, and she never, ever, ever wanted it to stop. He reached for the bottom of her T-shirt, to pull it over her head. Should she? Would she?

Hell, yes, she decided, and pulled the T-shirt off herself. Then she was in his arms again, his hands tangled in her hair, and he was kissing her the way she'd always dreamed of being kissed.

It happened so fast. Tom stood up. The next thing Kiley knew, Tom had lifted her in his arms as if she weighed nothing at all. *Thank God for all that farmwork,* she thought giddily; the guy was strong.

He carried her into the bedroom and gently laid her down atop his French silk burgundy quilt. He pulled off his own T-shirt, and Kiley was looking at the ripped abs that millions of girls had seen on a fifty-foot billboard on Sunset Avenue. They had wanted him. She, Kiley McCann of La Crosse, Wisconsin, had him.

He kissed down her stomach. Kiley shut her eyes dreamily. How many girls had Tom carried into this room, this bed? How many girls had he made moan and groan the way that girl—whoever she was—had moaned and groaned the night Kiley had been trying to sleep in the suite next door?

Her eyes popped open. She turned her head. Evidently some photos had slipped out of Tom's photo album, because two or three were strewn across his wooden nightstand. Lost in the bliss, Kiley didn't pay them any attention . . . until one caught her eye. Tom. With Marym. Their arms around each other, obviously a couple. Kiley sat up so quickly she practically knocked Tom off the bed.

"What?" he asked, obviously concerned.

"I . . . I . . . ." She gulped hard. "I don't think I'm ready for this."

Tom rolled over onto his back, one hand thrown behind his head and his hair flopping boyishly across his forehead; he looked about as perfect as a boy could look. He stared up at the ceiling. "I would have appreciated it if you'd told me a little sooner."

"I didn't know a little sooner."

Silence. He rolled toward her. "Okay, then."

"Really?"

"Yeah, of course, really," Tom said. "I want to make love to you, Kiley, but only when you want it to happen." He reached for a lock of her reddish brown hair. "Did something happen . . . ?"

Yes. Marym used to be your girlfriend, or maybe she's still your girlfriend. If I have sex with you, what will it mean? This is way too much, way too fast for me.

She didn't say any of that. Instead, she just said, "No, nothing."

Tom wrapped her in his arms. She felt his heart beating against hers. She realized she was probably the biggest idiot in the entire Los Angeles area for not going through with it.

Gee, she thought glumly, *Mom would be so proud.*

17

Thank God. They're all asleep.

Just like Kiley, as a rule, Esme did not drink. But after the day she had had with the twins and the boys from hell (as she'd decided to call Ham and Miles), she was craving a double shot of tequila. She sat in a beach chair at the ocean's edge, under the inky black subtropical night sky. One of the few clouds hid the moon. It was just her and the water; the warm waves coming ashore gently washed over her ankles. She knew there were four different places within five minutes' walk where she could get not just a double shot of tequila, but any other alcoholic concoction she could think of or the bartender could invent for her. The problem was, she was too damn tired to even think about moving.

The incident at the wacked-up relay had been just the beginning. There had been farting contests, food fights at lunch—

Ham had even faked his own drowning in an effort (largely successful) to freak Esme out. By midafternoon, when the boys were running off in different directions from their scheduled activity at the arts and crafts shed, taunting Esme to catch them, Esme had been wishing that she'd never been asked to come on this so-called vacation. The worst part of it was how the twins had been influenced by the Silverstein boys, instead of the other way around.

There was no possibility of complaining to the parents, either. The Goldhagens and the Silversteins had elected to go on an excursion to Dunns River Falls, supposedly the most beautiful waterfall on the island, and then to a reggae club in Ocho Rios that was apparently never frequented by tourists. Which was just so damn nice for them. At least someone was having fun—the someone certainly wasn't Esme. She had had to take charge of all four kids right through dinner (a disaster that had resulted in another food fight, this one involving curried goat) and then through after-dinner activities (Esme had reluctantly skipped the magic show for a kids' bingo game, where Ham had insisted he was the winner even though he wasn't, then flung his bingo chips at the social director). The only saving grace was that both sets of parents were willing to have their butlers stay on duty. Esme suspected that was only because they realized that if they gave her no free time at all, she might revolt.

"Hey."

She turned to the soft, Jamaican-inflected voice behind her, and recognized the male silhouette. It was Winston, the guy who'd run the wacked-up relay and so many other of the kids' activities since then. Though he'd spoken harshly to Esme at the pool, she had actually come to like the guy. He didn't have an easy job (she could relate), and he just did his best to do it well.

"Esme, right?" he asked.

"I was until today," Esme joked. "Now you can just call me exhausted."

Winston chuckled and knelt beside her. "I hear ya, girl," he agreed, letting his accent sing. "Tink-a me doin' it day after day, with all these spoiled American children. I try to keep up de good front, but dey don't know the meaning of ' 'nuff respect.' "

" 'Nuff respect?" Esme wasn't sure she'd heard correctly.

"It's an expression we use down here," Winston explained. "Means people are equal, I respect you if you respect me. Mind if I sit?" He indicated a beach chair that had been left out, maybe twenty feet away.

"Sure, join me," Esme said. She was happy for company that was over the age of nine, as long as Winston didn't expect a brilliant conversationalist.

He dragged the chaise closer and sat facing Esme. "Hope you don't mind. I saw you come down here and took de liberty of ordering— Ah, it looks like it is arriving. Hello, Kara!"

"Hello, Winston!" A smiling Jamaican woman carrying a tray above her head on her right hand and a folding table in her left came bounding down the beach, easily balancing both. "Ready for a midnight snack for two?"

"Perfect," Winston told her. "Thank you."

" 'Nuff respect," the tall, slender waitress replied as she expertly opened the folding table, then put her tray down on it. "Fresh prawns on ice, a cold artichoke with hollandaise and truffles, ackee in case your friend is adventurous, and a split of champagne on ice with two glasses. Enjoy, and have a wonderful evening here in Jamaica."

"What's ackee?" Esme asked as Kara departed. She suddenly realized how hungry she was, having spent more time at dinner being a cop than eating.

Winston laughed. "Sort of like our national fruit. But you don't eat the fruit. Just the part around the seeds. You cook it, that's why it looks like scrambled eggs. Try a quips."

Esme looked blank.

"A quips . . . that's patois for a little bit." Winston took a spoon and spooned up some ackee, then offered it to Esme.

She tasted it, letting the fruit roll around on her tongue before swallowing it. "It's delicious." She dug the spoon in and took another bite. "Do you think I can get ackee in Los Angeles?"

He poured champagne into the two flutes before he answered. "You so upful! I suppose so, at a West Indian market. You'd have to look."

"What does 'you so upful' mean?"

"You're an upbeat kind of girl," Winston intoned. He took a sip of the champagne. "Dom Perignon. Only the best for our guests. I can see I have to speak speaky-spoky wid you."

Esme laughed. "Sorry. No clue what you just said."

"Speaky-spoky means English that is talked in America," Winston explained. "When a friend goes to America and comes home speaking all proper, we say that's speaking speaky-spoky."

The prawns looked tasty. Esme took a whole one and popped it into her mouth. "We kind of have the same thing in the Echo," she told him. "Where I live. Well, where I grew up."

"Where you live now?" Winston asked.

"Just a sec, I'll tell you. Suddenly, I'm famished." After several more prawns, a few more bites of ackee, and some of the artichoke dipped in the heavenly hollandaise sauce, Esme found herself telling Winston the story of how she came to work for the Goldhagens and live at a huge estate in Bel Air.

What the hell, she thought. She'd never see this guy again after this so-called vacation was over. It was a pleasure too to be talking to an actual grown-up. That had been a rarity throughout the day.

As she finished her story, she saw Winston reach into his pocket. "You like a ganja?" He held up an enormous marijuana joint wrapped in thin white paper. "We call them spliffs."

Esme laughed. "So do we. When they're that big."

"You mind?" he asked.

"Umm . . . not really. But not for me."

Winston struck a match to the spliff, then lifted it to his lips and inhaled deeply. The bittersweet smell of Jamaica's finest filled the air.

"You sure you don't want some? This came from a cousin's property up in the Blue Hills. You'll be paying respects to my family."

"I don't think so," Esme said with a chuckle. "But you go ahead." She regarded him in the moonlight. "So, they don't mind if you hang out with the American nanny?"

"Not a-tall," Winston assured her, then exhaled a mouthful of ganja smoke, the fumes curling out his lips and into the ocean air. "Here in Jamaica, everyone has playtime."

"Well, I wish we had that philosophy in America." Esme

sighed. "My life is more like: the people I work for get playtime, I get kid time and kid overtime."

Winston threw his head back and his full-bodied laugh rang through the salty night air. Esme had enjoyed talking with him, and had a newfound appreciation for ackee. But hanging out with a Jamaican guy who was getting high on her *very* working vacation didn't seem like the best idea in the world. She didn't want to go back to the Goldhagens' vacation house smelling as if she'd turned into a Rastafarian, a member of that Jamaican religious sect for whom marijuana consumption was pretty much a more-than-once-a-day ritual.

"I should go," Esme said, swinging her legs around to the side of the chaise. "Thanks for the feast; it was great."

"My pleasure." He took another hit off his spliff. "How long you stayin'?"

Esme didn't actually know. The Goldhagens had been vague about how long the vacation would last, because Steven had a number of network pitch meetings for new show ideas. If one of those pitches had to be rescheduled, they might have to return to Los Angeles quickly. Of course, with the private jet, they were not at the mercy of the regular airlines' schedules. "A few more days," she said.

"Well, if you'd like to see some of the island, it would be my pleasure. I can tell you're not one of them," Winston told her.

"One of who?"

Winston grinned. "You know exactly what I'm talking about, girl. You're not one of them. You're one of us. 'Nuff respect, Esme. And good night."

"Thanks, Winston. You made my night. I mean it."

Winston saluted by taking one more deep toke; Esme headed up the beach toward the Goldhagens' house. The resort employee was right. She wasn't one of them, and never would be. This trip was driving that point home more than ever.

18

"Jeez, Lydia, what are you— Stop the car. Put your foot on the— No, the brake!" Billy bellowed.

Lydia slammed on the brakes of Billy's classic 1967 Mustang convertible, and the car stopped with a jerk so powerful that, but for the seat belt/shoulder harness combination, Lydia and Billy would easily have been thrown against the windshield.

Lydia smiled at him. "Okay, I stopped. Now what?"

"Now what?" Billy echoed. "Now you can find yourself a new driving teacher! You scared the hell out of me."

It was late the next morning, and Lydia was getting her first driving lesson, having picked up her permit earlier at the California Department of Motor Vehicles. Fortunately, Anya was taking Jimmy and Martina to the pediatrician for their annual checkups, followed by a visit to the dentist for their biannual cleaning. (Lydia wondered what there could possibly be for the dentist to clean. The children were permitted no sugar or soda, and had to brush their teeth with Sonicare electric toothbrushes when they woke up, after every meal, and before bedtime, plus floss to Anya's exacting standards. The biggest danger to their dental health, Lydia figured, was that the enamel of their teeth would be worn away by the time they each reached middle school.) The good news was, Lydia didn't have to be home for the children until after one o'clock. Then they were all going over to the country club.

Billy had decided that the expansive parking lots at Santa Monica College would be a great place for Lydia's first lesson. Since the college was on intersession, it was pretty much deserted. No pesky vehicles to get in Lydia's way.

Things had started out well, and Lydia had proved to be an apt pupil. Though she'd inched around the parking lot for the first few minutes, it wasn't long before she'd figured out how little she needed to turn the wheel for the power steering to kick in. She even tried to use her turn signals when she was going either right or left.

Twenty minutes into the lesson, Lydia asked the fateful question: "Can we go out on the street?"

Billy had been negative on the notion—it was too soon. But Lydia had cajoled and charmed him—between steamy kisses—assuring him that she really could handle it. Her final winning argument had involved a well-placed right hand on his left upper thigh, not to mention an eyeful of what was just underneath her secondhand Anna Sui eyelet top. Then she'd whispered in his ear: "Oh, Billy, I've killed a feral pig with my bare hands and I once drank goat piss during a shaman's learning ceremony—without throwing up, I might add. Do you really think I'm scared of Santa Monica Boulevard?"

Lydia personally suspected that it had been her hand on his thigh (or his sneak peek at the lace of her La Perla push-up bra), as opposed to her argument, that had nearly caused him to relent. She'd gunned the Mustang's engine—it roared with every one of its three-hundred-plus horsepower. Driving on the street was going to be much more fun than digging for grubs.

And then, just when Lydia figured she had spun her web perfectly, Billy had made her crazy by turning her down. "Another hour here. Maybe tomorrow, if you don't make any mistakes."

Oh, the boy was just maddening! He had way too much self-control about *everything*. Her eyes narrowed. If there was one thing Lydia hated, it was being told what to do. It made her think of a time when she was eleven and a couple of the Ama kids, Cuznco and Myrine, had invited her to go into the rain forest for a monkey hunt. She'd only ever been monkey hunting with one of the senior tribal leaders, never just with other kids.

When her father heard that there were going to be no adults on the hunt, he'd put his foot down (impressive, since his foot was clad in handwoven hemp sandals; his only pair of real shoes had been stolen by a tribal leader disgruntled about his wife's pregnancy—and Lydia's father's refusal to do anything about it). In any case, Lydia could not go on the hunt.

Myrine and Cuznco thought it was hilarious that Dr. Chandler wouldn't let Lydia come with them. Lydia found that horribly embarrassing; she told her dad that she was just going to go down the river to try to trap a yellow-spotted Amazon River turtle for dinner.

When Dad said fine, Lydia got her carefully whittled blowgun, tucked it into her clothes, and hiked into the rain forest by herself. For two hours, she crouched carefully in the jungle, waiting for the perfect target. She came back triumphant, not with a turtle, but with a fat squirrel monkey slung over her shoulder by its tail. She insisted on butchering it herself.

Needless to say, that was the last time her father forbade her to go hunting with her friends. Almost needless to say, Billy's telling her that she couldn't drive on the streets of Los Angeles seemed a minor setback compared to past parental decrees.

"Fine," Lydia chirped, not one to be thwarted so easily. "I'll simulate."

With that, she pushed the transmission into drive and zoomed across the parking lot. She cut the wheels this way and that, rounding one light stanchion, edging past a Dumpster with only inches to spare, reaching forty-five miles an hour at one stretch, and then braking to a perfect stop just before they slammed into a guard gate between the parking lot and Pico Boulevard.

That was when Billy shouted at her to stop the car and told her that she scared the hell out of him and she ought to get a new driving instructor.

She batted her eyelashes, which were normally pale blond like her hair but at the moment were coated with three layers of Black Night Denova Lash-Pump mascara, which was sold only in Australia and was so sought after that there was normally a three-month waiting list. Lydia had spied it atop a gift basket sent to her aunt from ESPN. Having recently read about the mascara in *Allure,* she was dying to try it. So she'd deftly extracted the mascara from underneath the gift basket's red cellophane cover, then rearranged the cellophane so that her aunt wouldn't be able to tell that anything was missing. Lydia reasoned that at least she would put the mascara to good everyday use; Aunt Kat wore it only when she was on camera.

"Oh, I know you still want to teach me. On the street. Right?"

Billy laughed. "You are one of a kind. You know that, don't you?"

"I do," Lydia answered solemnly. "I really do."

"I need a car," Lydia told Kiley. "Pronto."

She stretched in her chaise longue by the side of the family pool at the country club, enjoying the hot sun on her face. Lying out by the pool in a white Ralph Lauren bikini dotted with pink polo ponies while Jimmy and Martina frolicked in the water was a part of her nanny job at which she truly excelled. (She'd discovered the bikini in a bag of clothing in the basement that had been destined for Goodwill Industries—Anya's handwriting was on the masking tape label. It was just so Anya to give away a limited edition Ralph Lauren bikini. The woman had the fashion sense of a tapir.) Figuring that Anya was already giving these clothes away, she felt safe putting it on.

At the moment, her cousins were playing a water basketball game that had been organized by Nanny and Me, as were Kiley's kids, Star and Moon. Fortunately, there were too many nannies, so Lydia and Kiley had oh-so-graciously volunteered to sit this one out.

"It's not that easy," Kiley replied, reaching for the sunscreen. "First you have to pass a driver's test. Then you have to get enough money to buy the car."

"Details, details," Lydia proclaimed airily. She nodded her chin toward the pool. "Hey, check out our kids. They actually seem to be getting along."

Kiley rubbed sunblock into her freckled arms. "Star and Moon play well with others. And now we're at the end of the positive attributes list." Star's ballerina-lithe body was on full display in a bandeau bikini sprinkled with pink sequins. Moon thankfully wore a normal seven-year-old's baggy blue and green swimming trunks with a drawstring. Despite the vast alphabet of disorders his mom claimed Moon exhibited, he was splashing his sister playfully while she squealed in mock terror.

It was later the same day—Lydia had just filled Kiley in on her driving lesson with Billy on Santa Monica Boulevard, where, as she had predicted, she had done extremely well. It wasn't as if driving a car was an actual challenge. She peered at Kiley through the mock tortoiseshell J.Lo sunglasses the club had given all the nannies in their welcome baskets. "Wait, is that an actual new bathing suit?" she teased. "What happened to the ugly blue Speedo tank thing from *Platinum Nanny*?"

Kiley's new bathing suit was a baby blue one-piece with boy shorts (the better to rein in her butt, Kiley had declared) and a delicate halter top that slightly scooped to show her collarbones. The hand-tied halter fully displayed her back's creamy skin. It wasn't a Gottex original, Lydia decided, but it was a definite improvement.

"I was trying to cheer myself up," Kiley confessed. "Honestly, Lydia, working for Evelyn is a miserable experience."

"Times ten, by that look on your face," Lydia pronounced. She rolled onto her left hip and peered at Kiley. "You look like a hunter who just missed a wild boar with his last blow dart."

Kiley threw an arm over her forehead. "It's Tom."

"Really." Lydia conspiringly leaned closer. "Feel free to share."

Kiley sighed. "I went back to the hotel with him. To his suite."

"Uh-oh, I think I see where this is headed. The oh-so-hot Mr. Chappelle is oh-so-not between the sheets. Am I right?"

"Well, I wouldn't exactly know," Kiley confessed, "because I didn't exactly go through with it."

"Because?" Lydia prompted.

"Because I'm a wuss." Kiley smacked the palm of her hand against her forehead. "What is wrong with me? Everything was perfect. He was perfect! And I . . . I chickened out. I kept thinking about Marym—you know, his gorgeous, perfect, supermodel girlfriend."

"Past-tense girlfriend, right?"

"That's what I'm not sure about," Kiley replied glumly. "I saw a photo of them together. *Very* together."

Now *this* was getting interesting.

"So someone shot Tom and Marym having sex. Did you find it, or did he show it to you?"

Kiley threw her hand in the air. "Are you on drugs? Of course they weren't having sex in the picture."

"But you just said—"

"They had their arms around each other; obviously a couple," Kiley explained.

Lydia sat up and let this information settle for a moment. "So . . . you did not have sex with the boy of your dreams because you happened to see a photo of him with his arm around his former girlfriend? Have I got all the facts straight?"

"I know how stupid it sounds, believe me," Kiley lamented. "But remember how I told you I heard them through the wall during *Platinum Nanny,* before I ever met him—"

"Yuh. So?"

"So . . . she's perfect, Lydia. And I'm not! And . . . he had the lights on."

Lydia reached for her glass bottle of French Vittel water so that she could contemplate this information. She thought Kiley was nuts, of course, but was trying to learn to think before she spoke. "Well, I would say that you need to call that boy right now and set up an instant replay."

"Maybe I just don't belong with a guy that gorgeous. It makes me too self-conscious." Kiley sighed. "Did you and Billy hook up yet?"

"No," Lydia admitted. "But soon."

Kiley reached for her sunglasses. "Well, then I'd say neither one of us can speak from actual experience. Anyway, Tom hasn't called me since he dropped me off at Evelyn's, so it's probably over."

Even though Lydia thought that Kiley was probably insane, she reached for her hand in a moment of girlfriend solidarity. "I'm sorry, sweetie. Between that and the kiddies—"

"Oh, not just the kiddies," Kiley corrected. "Evelyn is certifiable. She does primal scream therapy."

"Which is?"

"It's— Oops, I think Jimmy just got a ball in his eye. Or a finger."

Lydia turned. Jimmy was holding his right eye with both hands and moaning. Since the game was continuing around him, it didn't look too serious.

"Supernanny to the rescue." She rose from the chaise. "Can you do one little thing for me, Kiley?"

"Sure. You want me to get some ice or something?"

"I want you to go stand in the breezeway between this pool and the adult pool." She pointed toward the far end of the family pool, beyond the lifeguard stand. "Stop at the snack bar first and get a tall iced tea in a glass."

"Why?" Kiley asked.

"Gotta be iced tea and gotta be in a tall glass," Lydia repeated.

"Why don't you just order one from the waiter?" Kiley asked, bewildered.

"Oh, it's not for me," Lydia assured her. "I'll keep an eye on your kidlets."

"Lydia—"

"Trust me on this," Lydia insisted, smiling sweetly. "This is about to change your life."

Kiley felt like a complete idiot, standing alone in the breezeway between the two pools with a tall glass of iced tea in her right hand. She could hear the chortles and yells of the kids in the family pool—Jimmy's eye had turned out to be a momentary victim of a teammate's flinging fingers, but he'd already gotten back into the game. To her right was the adult pool, with its pockets of celebrities playing poker, reading scripts, and doing deals; or actresses/new moms sporting teeny-tiny bikinis to demonstrate that they'd recovered their figures after childbirth.

At the bar where she'd purchased her iced tea (well, Evelyn had purchased it, since Kiley told them to put it on Evelyn's tab. That had been her deal with Platinum, though Evelyn hadn't said anything about it at all), she'd recognized Eddie Murphy with two young African American women in white crocheted bikinis, so stunningly beautiful that they didn't look real. Various players from the L.A. Lakers—white, black, and Latino, all of them six foot eight or taller—were laughing loudly from their towel-covered chaises.

She sipped her tea and enjoyed the heady scent from the eucalyptus trees soaring high above her, the planters nestled in circular cutouts in the aqua-tiled path.

Kiley was just about to depart when she noticed a thin, blond woman—was there any other kind in Los Angeles, she wondered—staring at her intently from the far end of the breezeway. She wore a sage green Tracy Reese tunic, Juicy Couture white linen pants, and golden beaded Indian slippers. Ropes of bracelets snaked her arms. She looked about thirty years old, and was vaguely familiar.

The woman waved once. Kiley turned to look behind her, but there was no one else there. She turned back. Then, like some parody of an espionage movie, the woman edged behind the eucalyptus tree closest to Kiley and crooked a finger slyly in her direction.

Before Kiley could stop herself, she laughed out loud. She had no idea what was going on, but whatever it was seemed ridiculous. What the hell; she was at the Brentwood Hills Country Club. It couldn't hurt to just talk to the woman. She went over and introduced herself.

"I'm Kiley McCann. I don't know you, do I?"

The woman looked right, then left. "Beth Paulson. You're a nanny, right?"

"Right," Kiley acknowledged. Beth reached out a perfectly

manicured hand with OPI ballet-slipper pink nails for Kiley to shake.

"Do you know who I am?" Beth asked.

"You look kind of familiar," Kiley admitted, "but sorry, no."

"*The Dispatcher?* On FX?" Beth prompted.

"Umm . . ." Kiley was a little embarrassed to admit that back in Wisconsin, her family didn't have cable because they couldn't afford it. "Umm . . . I can't say I've ever watched. Do you have something to do with that show?"

Beth giggled. "It's the highest-rated show on cable right now. About a nine-one-one dispatcher who gets psychic flashes about her calls?"

Now that Kiley thought about it, she had vaguely heard of the show; maybe it had been mentioned on *Entertainment Tonight* or something like that.

"I play the dispatcher," Beth explained. "My husband, Dirk, is executive producer. So, Kiley. Lovely name." She offered Kiley a radiant smile, showing off the perfect, Chiclet-white teeth that screamed "porcelain veneers at a thousand dollars a tooth!" "Who are you working for?"

"Evelyn Bowers. You probably don't know her, she's a pub—"

Beth exploded in laughter. "Evelyn Bowers? That nut job?"

"I don't know if she's a nut job." Kiley found herself defending her boss, which was ridiculous because, in fact, Kiley *did* think Evelyn was a nut job, but it didn't really seem right to dis the woman who employed her.

"I have a feeling you're being kind. Evelyn is famous here for abusing her nannies."

Huh. Kiley hadn't known that, obviously.

"The whole membership here knows Evelyn. She does

publicity for the tobacco industry, do you know that? How can she even sleep at night?"

Good point. On the other hand, growing up, Kiley had heard over and over again from her mom: if you don't have something nice to say about someone, keep your mouth shut. So she kept her mouth shut.

"What's it like working for her?" Beth prompted.

"It's . . . okay."

Beth gave Kiley a knowing look. "You haven't been with her for very long, have you."

Kiley allowed as how that was true.

"In the past three months, that woman has gone through six nannies—and those are only the ones I know about! They all either quit or got fired within a week or two."

Kiley bit her Bonne Bell Lip Smackered lip nervously. "I didn't know that."

Beth nodded. "It's so smart of you to look around before the situation gets totally out of control. I've heard stories. . . . Well, it's just really bad."

Kiley was still stuck on the "It's so smart of you to look around" part of what Beth had said. "Did you think that I'm looking for a job?" she asked.

Beth pushed her gold-rimmed Ray-Ban aviator sunglasses higher up on her head. "Everyone knows that nannies looking to jump stand in the breezeway holding a tall iced tea."

Kiley was in a state of shock. "They do? I mean . . . I, uh . . ." She had no idea what to say. So *that* was why Lydia had told her to stand there with drink in hand. "Well, you sure turned up fast. I just got here."

"Lucky me!" Beth chirped. "The only reason I'm looking is because my nanny of three years just eloped and moved to Vegas."

"I worked for Platinum," Kiley heard herself pitching.

"That was you?" Beth grabbed Kiley's wrist. "Oh my God, I know all about you. Platinum told everyone about her perfect nanny—before they carted her away to rehab, anyway. You're hired—"

"Hold it," Kiley forced herself to say. "It's not . . . that simple. We need to talk."

"Well, of course. Can I bring my husband into the conversation? He just came off the golf course; he's probably having a drink in the clubhouse. Let me call him."

Without waiting for Kiley to give the okay, she pressed the walkie-talkie feature on her Nokia cell phone that seemingly materialized out of nowhere. Five minutes later, a handsome Asian American guy—this was a surprise to Kiley, though she realized quickly that she shouldn't have automatically assumed Beth's husband would be white—with a shaved head and the build of an athlete stepped into the breezeway. She could see a platinum Rolex gleaming on his wrist as took his hands out of his khaki pockets.

"Down here, honey," Beth called.

Dirk Paulson looked genuinely happy to see his wife; he kissed her cheek. "Hey, sweetie."

Beth quickly filled Dirk in on possibly hiring Kiley as their nanny.

Dirk nodded. "Sounds good. What would you like to know about us?"

"Um . . . how many children do you have?"

"Just one," Beth replied. "She's a sweetheart. Her name is Grace. We named her after the church where we got married."

Kiley was impressed. "How old is she?"

"Eleven. She's such a sweet kid. Gets along with everyone, Girl Scout troop star, straight-A student, ace soccer player," Beth went on. "You can meet her; she's at the arts and crafts center right now."

"She's also quite a terrific young sculptor," Dirk chimed in proudly.

Kiley didn't know what to say. She was, frankly, dazzled. Was it possible that she had just lucked into what was apparently the most stable family in Los Angeles? Long-married parents who loved and respected each other, with only one child, named after their church. This was so different from Platinum or from Evelyn Bowers, so different from the Goldhagens or even Lydia's aunt and her partner.

Here in the divorce capital of the universe, Beth and Dirk were apparently a revelation from heaven.

"I'm interested," Kiley confessed. "But there are some . . . issues to work out, I think."

Dirk smiled. "With Evelyn Bowers? Don't worry, Kiley. First of all, if the issues are financial, whatever she's paying you, we'll beat it by a hundred bucks per week. If there's anything else, we've got it covered, too. Sometimes these situations require the new family to compensate the old family if there's been any financial, er, investment."

Better and better.

"Where do you guys live?" Kiley asked.

"Well, I have to admit I saw you out at the pool with Kat Chandler's nanny," Beth confessed. "Are you friends with her?"

"She's one of my best friends in Los Angeles, actually."

Beth and Dirk smiled at each other. "We don't know Kat and her partner very well, but we definitely know what they drive," Dirk said.

Beth gave her husband an arch look. "Dirk, stop being so cryptic. Kiley definitely is in luck." She smiled at Kiley. "You see, we live two houses down the canyon from Kat and Anya."

19

"Hi. Remember me?"

Lydia looked up from the issue of *Vogue* that she'd purloined from the ladies' room in the main dining room to see the cute golf pro from Costa Rica, Luis what-was-his-name. He was dressed in the same regulation club golf shirt as the day before, this time with sparkling white trousers.

She smiled. "Sure do. But let me put on my sunglasses before your pants blind me."

Luis indicated the chaise longue where Kiley had been sitting before she'd gone off to the breezeway. Lydia peeked over toward the breezeway again, where Kiley was deep in conversation with a blond woman and an Asian man. Then her eyes slid to the kids in the pool, all blessedly occupied with their water basketball.

Lydia was a girl who knew the fine art of listening in on

others' conversations without seeming to do it. She'd picked up the scuttlebutt around the club—the breezeway was the place where prospective employers could poach possible nannies who were unhappy with their current employers, and where unhappy nannies could go to be poached. In other words, it was the nanny-employer version of a pickup bar. Not that Lydia had ever been to a pickup bar. But she'd read a great exposé on one in *Cosmo* the year before.

She didn't tell Kiley this—she didn't want to give her a chance to back out. Sometimes, a friend had to do for another friend what that friend wouldn't do for herself.

Luis perched on the end of Kiley's chaise. "When am I going to be able to get you out on the golf course?"

She studied him a moment. "Well, it's a little tempting, in that you are very good-looking," she admitted. "However, I'd prefer to stare at you at an alternate locale."

Luis laughed. "I'm flattered. I think. Anyway, golf is one of the world's great games."

Lydia shook her head. "I don't think so. Who'd want to chase a little white ball around a park when they could just walk in that park wherever they wanted to go?"

"What would you prefer to do?"

"During the day? Make money. During the night?" She shrugged. "Use your imagination."

"I don't need to," Luis told her. "You're a beautiful girl. All I have to do is look at you. Who needs imagination?"

"A girl who chewed roasted bugs as snacks," she replied, quite honestly.

He made a face. "You chew—?"

"In a previous incarnation," she told him, not wanting to delve into her past. She glanced over at the pool again. Happy, playing kiddies. If only her job could be like this all the time. "So, Luis. Where were we?"

He cocked his head at her, a bemused look on his face. "So, besides ingesting cockroaches, what else do you like to do?"

Lydia stretched lazily, the Ralph Lauren bikini showcasing all the right places. "Lots of things. Clubbing, driving fast."

Luis grinned. "A girl after my own heart. What do you drive?"

Why did the boy want *details*?

"A cherry red Lamborghini," she replied.

Luis's eyes lit up. "You have a—"

"No," she confessed. "That would be in my dreams. Stuck here in the real world, the truth is . . . I don't actually have a car. I'm looking for one, though."

"Really," Luis said. "What are you in the market for? What's your price range?"

Lydia shifted uncomfortably on the chaise. "Um . . . that would be between free and . . . free?"

He laughed, and she swatted at his bicep. "I'm a nanny, for God's sake. I don't make any money. I'll settle for anything that runs."

Luis folded his arms. Lydia couldn't help noticing how nicely his biceps bulged. "I think you might be in luck."

"How so?"

"I just won a tournament in Las Vegas—satellite tour, not the real PGA, but the first-place prize was a car plus some money. So I've got this brand-new Toyota MR2 Spyder."

"And you're giving it to me?" Lydia squealed, even though she had zero idea what a Toyota MR2 Spyder looked like.

He put his hands over his heart. "Ouch. Sorry, no, I can't. But—"

"But what?" Lydia demanded. "I'm very happy for your new driving experience, but it doesn't help mine any."

He ran a hand across his cleft chin. "Tell you what. I'll give you a ride. And we can talk about your 'driving experience.' "

"If you let me drive it too, it's a deal," she said.

Luis stuck out his hand for Lydia to shake. "Deal."

"Great." Lydia didn't mention that she'd only been driving for approximately two hours, and that those two hours had taken place that very morning. She also didn't mention that she had a boyfriend. It wasn't as if she and Luis were going out on a *date*. "When?"

"What are you doing this evening?" Luis asked. "Say . . . around eight?"

Lydia thought for a moment. Work ended for her that day at 7:30 p.m. Billy had to work overtime. Again. Which meant her schedule was wide open.

"Around eight, I'd say you're picking me up in your hot new wheels," Lydia told him.

"Excellent," he agreed. "We'll drive by my place—"

She made a time-out T with her hands. "Hold on, buddy. How did we get from my place to your place so fast?"

"I meant behind my place," Luis explained. "There's something I want to show you. I promise to keep both hands on the wheel at all times."

All righty, then. He'd pick her up at eight.

The ride across the island of Jamaica had been hellacious, because there hadn't been a helicopter available on short notice that could carry five adults and four children. Instead, Steven and Diane had chartered a minivan with a Jamaican driver for the day; the concierge at Northern Look had assured them that the trek to the south coast of the island, to a place called St. Catherine, would take only a couple of hours.

This trip had been completely unplanned. However, when Steven and Diane had awakened that morning, they'd turned on a local radio station on their Bang & Olufsen clock radio. Between reggae songs, the deejay had done an on-air promotion for something called the Jamaican Sugarcane Cutting Championships, to take place that afternoon in this place called St. Catherine, at a cricket field (cricket was the most popular sport in Jamaica after soccer) converted into a festival grounds.

Steven and Diane immediately decided that this would be a fun way to spend the day; the Silversteins had agreed without hesitation . . . which was why Esme had to endure a nausea-inducing, bumpy ride from the north coast up through the hills, past the crowded, poor town of Moneague and the teeming Linstead market, and then down into Spanish Town and the sprawling St. Catherine Parish. The one saving grace to the ride was that the minivan had a DVD player. Esme had thought to borrow *The Karate Kid* and *Brother Bear* from the Northern Look collection before they departed. Though Ham and his brother clamored for *Mortal Kombat,* the DVDs kept the noise in the back of the van down to a manageable level.

It wasn't hard to find the sugarcane cutting competition: there were dozens of hand-drawn signs on the main road that led to the cricket pitch. The driver parked their van in a crowded, muddy parking lot, and the whole group of nine trooped to the stadium gate. This was nothing like Dodger Stadium, Esme saw as she approached. It was more like a high school football field, with two sets of bleachers and a high fence that circled the field. As they neared the gate, city buses from the capital city of Kingston were disgorging hundreds of passengers who'd decided to make a day trip of it.

"Be careful with the children," Diane cautioned Esme, who was grasping Weston with one hand and Easton with the other. Esme was trying to work up the nerve to ask Diane if she really had to watch the Silverstein kids all the time. She'd been thinking about it ever since she'd met the little brats, but she'd been too afraid to say anything. Well, she was *still* afraid. But she was beginning to deeply resent the patently unfair situation. No one had asked her; it had just been expected. The Silverstein kids were much more than double her workload.

Esme cleared her throat. "Diane, I was wondering if we could talk."

"Sure," Diane said easily.

Esme's heart pounded. She took a deep breath. Inhale. Exhale. "Well, I was wondering if I have to be responsible for watching Ham and Miles too? I mean, I will if I have—"

Diane cut her off with a wave of her hand. "Of course not. Actually, I was thinking about broaching this myself and it just slipped my mind. Now that I have a chance to think about it, it was very unfair what we did to you, saddling you with Erin and Peter's children."

Esme was shocked that Diane had already come to the same conclusion. On the other hand, it struck her as ironic that talking about it had "slipped Diane's mind." While it meant a lot to Esme, it wasn't much more than an afterthought to Diane.

"I've seen how Miles and Ham act," Diane continued.

"They're brats. They don't respect you, they don't respect us, and they don't respect themselves. To tell you the truth, I'm ashamed that Erin and Peter would drink mojitos on the beach while their children are such an embarrassment. Most of all, I don't like the way they influence the girls' behavior."

Esme nodded, but didn't chime in with her heartfelt agreement. It was one thing for Diane to insult the children of her friends, and quite another for the nanny to do so.

Diane put her hand atop Esme's. "In fact, you'd be doing me a favor if you'd keep my girls away from those boys."

Excellent.

"Will do," Esme agreed.

They reached the turnstiles to the cricket field. Steven bought tickets for everyone; then they were inside.

What a scene. On a stage by the scoreboard, a reggae band pounded out an infectious beat. In a circle around the field, there were dozens of booths set up, selling everything from colorful pastel paintings and hand-whittled masks to bottles of Red Stripe and fresh vegetable patties filled with well-seasoned callaloo. There were hordes of children gathered around games of chance and a face-painting booth; the minute Weston and Easton spotted the face painting, they clamored to have their faces decorated by the young Jamaican woman who was deftly stroking her brush on the children's cheeks.

"Go ahead," Steven told her. "We'll be . . ."

He looked around and saw a fenced-in area not far from where they'd come into the cricket grounds. It separated some tables with tablecloths from the rest of the festival. The people inside the fence were of mixed ethnicities—brown, white, black—as opposed to the crowd out here in the festival area itself, which was 99.9 percent black.

"Over there," he continued, and checked his watch. "How about in an hour?"

"Sounds good," Esme told him. Now that she had to look after only Easton and Weston, she felt positively giddy.

"Have fun," Steven said, and took out his wallet. "Here's some money. Keep a close eye on the girls; this is a madhouse. Bye, girls!"

He kissed his daughters, pressed some bills into Esme's hand, and waved goodbye. As soon as he was gone, the girls again begged to have their faces painted. Esme grinned. She couldn't wait to see how the girls' faces would turn out. Not only that, she was free of Ham and Miles. Not just for the rest of the stay in Jamaica, but forever.

While Weston and Easton sat happily on two low stools in the face-painting booth, attended to by the Jamaican girl who'd agreed to do them both at the same time and sworn to keep them chained to their chairs for the duration of their art project, Esme wandered over to a small exhibit directly next to her booth that explained the history of the sugar crop in Jamaica and the process by which it was harvested. She'd had no idea it was such strenuous work. Though machines did some of it, much of the Jamaican cane harvest was still done by hand, by incredibly strong men wielding machetes that were as thick as their forearms. Evidently, the night before the cane was cut, the fields were set on fire—the idea was to burn off the leaves and the outer coating of the cane plants, which grew eight to ten feet high. The fires burned hot and quick, leaving the cane behind.

The next day, the men moved through the fields, followed by flatbed pickup trucks, to gather the cut cane. Each man, if he was skilled enough and strong enough, could cut upwards of fifteen tons of cane a day. The work was backbreaking and dirty, all the more so because the night's fire left a sooty coating on the remaining cane. Yet the men would compete fiercely to cut the most cane, and they were paid by the weight of the cane they did cut. Today, the best cutter of the year would be honored; the award came with a five-thousand-dollar bonus prize.

At the far end of the exhibit were some sugarcane stalks and an actual machete, so that festival-goers could get a sense of what it was like to actually wield the blade and slash through some cane.

"You want to try?" A smiling man wearing jeans and nothing else—no shoes, no hat, no nothing—offered the machete to Esme. From the soot on his skin, Esme realized that he was one of the cane cutters. "It's good exercise," he told her in a lilting Jamaican accent, a huge grin splitting his dark face.

Esme snuck a glance back at the girls. Their faces were nearly done. "No, sorry, I've got to check on my kids," she confessed.

"Root for me, pretty girl," the man told her. "I'm Michael. I could really, really use the money."

"I will," Esme promised, then hurried back to the girls. They were grinning wildly as the artist held up a mirror for them to see her handiwork. Weston's face had been painted green, yellow, and black (the colors of the Jamaican flag), while Easton had a rising sun coming up from her chin, with rays of the sun radiating toward her eyes and ears. The work was, frankly,

162

stunning. A tattoo artist herself, Esme knew how hard it was to work with living canvases.

"Great," Esme told the artist. "What do I owe you?"

"You are American," she said. "I can tell from your accent. Do you have American dollars?"

Steven had given Esme the local Jamaican currency. But she saw the hungrily hopeful look on the artist's face; evidently American money was worth more to her. Well, she had some of her own money in her back pocket. So she nodded, hoping she could cover the cost. As long as it was under forty dollars, she was okay. And she was certain that Steven would reimburse her.

"How about . . . seven dollars for the both of them?" the artist ventured. "Unless you think that is too much."

On the Santa Monica Pier, it would cost three times that much, Esme realized.

"How about seven dollars for each of them?" Esme countered. "You did a wonderful job."

"That is very, very generous of you," the artist said. "You are lucky to live in America. I want to go to art school there. But I cannot get a visa. They will not give a visa to a poor Jamaican girl. I know it is a crazy dream, but why should a girl not have dreams?"

Esme's heart went out to the girl; she handed her a twenty-dollar bill. "Please, keep it all," she said. "Isn't there a place for you to study art here?"

The girl laughed sadly. "You do not know much about our island, do you?"

"Not really," Esme admitted.

"We have no real art school in Jamaica. There is the University of the West Indies, but I cannot afford the tuition."

"Well, couldn't you get some kind of . . . student visa to

study in America?" Esme wondered aloud. Obviously the girl was very talented. There had to be a solution.

"Don't you understand me?" The artist's dark eyes bore into Esme's. "Don't you understand how lucky you are to be in America, to be an American citizen?"

"I do," Esme agreed. "But please understand, things aren't perfect in America, either."

The artist shook her head, the beads in her heavily braided hair swishing gracefully across her face. "Not perfect, maybe. That will happen only in heaven. Cuba is sixty miles from here. Do you see people in boats trying to go to Cuba? Or to Mexico? No! Everyone wants to go to America."

Esme gulped. The desire in this girl's voice was palpable. It was also coupled with a sort of resignation, a knowledge that no matter how much she wanted to go to America, to get the art training she craved, it was never going to happen.

I want to go to art school too, Esme thought. *I never even considered that I wouldn't be able to go if I wanted to.*

On their way across the island, she'd seen the ramshackle shacks so many poor Jamaicans lived in. Compared to that, the Echo was paradise. Esme was hit with a pang of guilt. It was all so relative, wasn't it: opportunity, prosperity, poverty. . . .

"It is too bad you are not a man," the artist joked. "Then you could marry me. That is sort of my last hope." She cleared her throat. "Not like I'm going to meet a rich American guy here, though."

"Well . . ."

Esme didn't know what to say. This was a very uncomfortable conversation, mostly because there was absolutely nothing she could do to help this nice girl. She prided herself on being competent—so much more competent than the rich girls of Beverly Hills and Bel Air, who ran to the manicurist when they chipped a nail and thought nothing of spending eight bucks on a caffe latte when they could just as easily brew a cup of Folgers at home. Yet here she was, with a situation over which she had no control and about which she could do nothing. She didn't know this girl. In fact, she didn't even know her name . . . but she felt a kinship with her.

"What's your name?" Esme asked.

"Tarshea," the girl said. "Tarshea Manley."

"I'm glad to meet you, Tarshea," Esme told her, shaking the girl's hand. "I hope that . . ."

Esme froze—it was as if time froze too. She was looking over Tarshea's shoulder at the stools where the twins had been sitting.

The kid-sized stools were empty.

Esme wheeled around, looking in every direction. Hordes of people were milling about, laughing, cheering, and chomping on sugarcane. But none of them was Easton or Weston.

The girls were gone.

20

Kiley had quickly gone with the Paulsons down to arts and crafts and had met their daughter, Grace. She was, as described, lovely, with long copper hair, a smattering of freckles across her upturned nose, and her dad's almond-shaped eyes. She showed Kiley two sculptures she was working on, one of a pony and another an abstract mass of semicircles and oblong blobs; Grace charmed her by saying she was trying to sculpt "laughter." She decided on the spot to accept the Paulsons' job offer.

She hurried back to Star and Moon at the pool, figuring out her plan. By the time she'd brought them home, she pretty much knew how she was going to proceed. She was not going to be an ass about it. She would resign that evening, but she'd give Evelyn a week's notice. Since she'd been there for less than five days, this seemed more than fair.

Unfortunately, the Hollywood grapevine extended to the nanny network. By the time Kiley parked Evelyn's Vibe in the driveway,

166

Evelyn had already heard the news. Kiley didn't know how. That she had been informed was obvious: Evelyn stood in the doorway, her bony arms folded against her tangerine cashmere T-shirt, her mouth an angry slash across her face.

"How dare you!" she bellowed at Kiley, even before her children got inside. "You little two-timing user!"

Kiley's jaw fell open. She had no idea what to say. Star and Moon stared up at her; Moon picked his nose and smeared the booger on his sister. Kiley had anticipated that Evelyn might be upset when she told her; she had even anticipated an upbraiding. But she hadn't expected to be labeled a two-timing user.

"I'm sorry, Evelyn." Kiley tried to calm her boss.

"What did she do, Mom?" Moon asked eagerly.

"You should take her upstate, like they did to that girl on *The Sopranos,*" Star added.

"You should be sorry," Evelyn shot back. "I saved your ass, and this is how you thank me? By quitting?"

Moon figured out what was going on. "You mean Kiley quit?" He started jumping up and down. "Hurray! Hurray! Kiley is a big fat bitch, she's the biggest bitch in the whole wide world!" he sang. "She's a super bitch, she's the biggest bi—"

"Moon! Go in the house!" Evelyn thrust a forefinger toward the front door.

"No! Let's have a party!"

"Moon!" Evelyn was furious. Meanwhile, Kiley watched Star slink away toward the back entrance of the house, though she did turn around to give Kiley the finger.

"Party, party!" Moon cried, running in circles. "Kiley's quitting! Woo-hoo! Woo-hoo!"

"In the house!" Evelyn ordered again, then fixed angry eyes on Kiley. "Do you see how upset my child is? Do you see what you've done?"

What I've done? "I appreciate the opportunity you gave me." During the drive home, Kiley had mentally rehearsed what she would say. "Sometimes these things just don't work out, and—"

"I'm a publicist, Kiley. I make up lines of shit like that. I packed your bags. They're in the garage. Just do me one last favor."

"Sure, Evelyn, if I can—"

"Oh, you can. *Get the hell out of my face!*"

With that, Evelyn turned and slammed the door to her house.

"And thank you very much, too," Kiley muttered. She trudged off to the garage to get her bags, thinking that Evelyn had a lot of nerve to go into her room and pack them up.

What to do now? Call the Paulsons and see if I can start immediately. Then call Tom to see if he can take me over there.

But Tom hadn't called her since their aborted sexcapade in his hotel suite. Who knew if he'd ever call again? She simply didn't have the nerve to call him. She couldn't call Lydia because Lydia didn't drive. And she couldn't call Esme because Esme was in Jamaica.

She'd have to call a cab. Damn.

Esme's breath came in rasps as she tore into the thick crowd in the center of the infield, shouting frantically in Spanish for the twins. "Weston! Easton! *¿Dónde estáis? ¡Ven acá! ¡Ven acá! ¿Dónde estáis?*"

She looked left and right, but all she saw were unfamiliar

black faces—happy festival-goers drinking beer and smoking the occasional spliff, faces looking at her curiously as she yelled out in Spanish. There was a children's dance troupe performing in the center of the field, and Esme cut through the watching crowd, shouting for the children. Nothing; only puzzled looks from people having a wonderful time.

Then she heard her own name being called, but by an adult's voice instead of a child's. "Esme? What are you looking for? Esme?"

Esme turned. The artist Tarshea, who had painted the girls' faces, was coming toward her at a dead run.

"What's the matter?" Tarshea demanded.

"The girls! They're gone!" Esme heard the hysteria in her own voice. "Oh God!"

"Stop," Tarshea told her, taking Esme by the shoulders. "Calm yourself. We will do no good finding them if you are a wreck. Now, they are little. They cannot have gone far. Let us— Wait. I know what we should do." She started pulling Esme toward the stage.

"What are you doing?" Esme demanded.

"We go to the band, we use their microphone and make an announcement to the crowd. The children will come right to us," Tarshea explained. "You have not been listening, there have been announcements from there the whole afternoon."

For a brief second, Esme felt a bit of hope instead of abject panic. Then she thought of Steven and Diane Goldhagen, wherever they were at the festival, and what they would hypothetically hear from the stage.

"We have two lost children, Easton and Weston Goldhagen. They are Colombian and have painted faces. If you see Weston and Easton

Goldhagen, please bring them to their apparently imcompetent nanny by the left side of the main stage. Kidnappers, please resist the urge to snap up this golden opportunity. Thank you very much."

Oh my God. She would be so fired.

"No!" Esme said quickly. "No announcement. Not yet."

"But it is the best way to find the children," Tarshea protested.

"No. Wait," Esme pleaded, her voice cracking from the strain.

She knew the right thing to do would be to send Tarshea up to the stage to make the announcement about the girls while she ran over and found Steven and Diane. The longer that she waited to tell them, the worse the consequences would be. It would be bad enough that the girls were lost somewhere in this sunbaked field of sweaty humanity, in a country not their own, where no one spoke their first language. If Steven and Diane figured out that the girls were lost and Esme hadn't told them right away, there'd be no hope, even if Esme threw herself at their mercy.

"Okay, five minutes," Tarshea reluctantly agreed. "You go to the left, I go to the right. We will meet back here—so that way, we cover everything twice. Five minutes. I'll see you then."

Esme headed to the left. The good news was that it was the opposite direction from where the Goldhagens were—presumably, although her heart pounded even more when she realized that Steven and Diane could be anywhere in this crowd, and there was no reason to believe that they would have stayed in the place with the white tablecloths. The bad news was, there had to be at least ten thousand people crowded into the cricket grounds, the reggae band was wailing, people were partying and dancing everywhere. How in the world was she going to find five-year-old twins?

She sent up a quick prayer: *Please, at least let them be together out there. Somewhere.*

In the five minutes it took her to orbit the cricket grounds, she looked everywhere she could think of, putting herself in the mind of the girls: What would they be interested in? What would keep their attention? So when she came to an area where kids could ride on the backs of goats, she lingered for a few moments; lots of kids, none of them hers. At a game contest that was a variation on ringtoss, except the game was designed to allow kids to win and let them throw hula hoops over full bottles of soda—if the kid won, the kid got the soda. But no Weston or Easton.

Time was running out; she was breathing so hard she was afraid she might hyperventilate. Looking this way and that, wiping the sweat from her brow with a forearm, cutting and dodging around people without saying excuse me, practically knocking over an elderly gentleman with a cane who was eating a plateful of oxtail and roast potatoes.

"Weston!" Esme shouted. "Easton?"

No response, just the roar of the crowd answering something that the reggae band's lead singer had shouted into his microphone. She realized she'd worked her way all around the field. As she did, Tarshea came running from the opposite direction.

"No children?" she asked.

Esme shook her head.

"You need to make the announcement, now," Tarshea urged.

"Fine," Esme agreed. It no longer mattered to her if she lost her job; all that mattered to her was those two little girls. What if someone found out they were the children of a very rich, very famous American? They could be held for ransom, or worse.

Please, God; please, God; please, God, she prayed as she sprinted for the stage behind Tarshea, who was boldly yelling at people to get out of the way, this was an emergency, she had to get to the stage. Though the area in front of the stage was wall-to-wall dancers, Tarshea's insistent voice was undeniable. Everyone stepped aside so that Esme and Tarshea could pass. Then Tarshea ducked under a thick rope and helped Esme under it, and the two of them were backstage.

"We wait for the song to finish, then we talk to the stage manager," Tarshea decreed.

Esme nodded. It was all she could manage. The prayer kept repeating itself in her brain: *Please, God.*

And then, as if she was divinely inspired, she got an idea.

The song ended, and Esme stood by while Tarshea had a quick consultation with the guy who was in charge, a huge man with a huge belly, who was sweating profusely under a black, yellow, and green wool cap. When they were done talking, the big man motioned to Esme.

"You go up there and take the center mike, say what you need to say," he instructed.

It was now or never.

Esme edged out onto the stage, hoping against hope both that the girls were within earshot and that her bosses were otherwise engaged. She reached the center of the stage, where the lead singer of the reggae band—a skinny guy with huge dreads—looked at her quizzically.

"Okay?" She pointed to the mike. "I've got to make a quick announcement."

The singer shrugged. "Yah mon, you do what you need to do."

"Escúchame, por favor. Si tú, Weston, y tú, Easton, puedes oir mi voz, escuches por favor mí. Llévese por las manos y la caminata a través de la muchedumbre a dónde la venda musical está jugando. Tú me verás en la etapa. Ahora ven. ¡Por favor!"

Basically, she begged—in Spanish, so that there was a vague chance that the Goldhagens wouldn't understand her—for Weston and Easton to come to the stage if they could hear the sound of her voice. Unless the Goldhagens were listening closely, their daughters' names in the midst of the rapid-fire Spanish might not even register with them. That was her hope, anyway.

Esme scanned the crowd, praying for a response to her announcement, praying that little two girls with painted faces would run up to her and throw their arms around her, and the Goldhagens would be none the wiser.

Esme stood there and waited. And waited. But no two little faces appeared.

21

Steven and Diane Goldhagen raced through the crowd at a dead run. Steven's face was contorted with anger and concern; Diane had tears running down her cheeks. The reggae band's lead singer was in the process of moving Esme off the stage in order to start a new song, so Esme didn't see her bosses until Steven slammed his hand down on the wooden stage with all his might.

So much for hoping that they wouldn't understand the Spanish.

"Esme, what the hell is going on here?" Steven bellowed.

"I—I—" Esme stammered.

"Where are the children?" Diane demanded, her voice rising an octave in fear. *"Where are my children?"*

Her panicky voice made Esme's stomach lurch. "I don't exactly—"

"Goddammit, Esme." Steven jumped up onto the stage to grab her by the arms. "Tell me you didn't lose the children out there in that . . . mess!"

Diane wrapped her arms around herself. "Oh God, oh God . . ."

Steven pointed at the Jamaican in the wool cap. "Call security. Now!" he bellowed.

"Esme!"

They all turned. There stood Tarshea, holding Easton's and Weston's hands.

"I'm so sorry, Esme," Tarshea said, "I should have told you that I was taking them to another spot to finish their face painting. There was a color I wanted. You must be the most responsible nanny in history to come up here and make that announcement."

Weston and Easton smiled, and Esme realized that they didn't understand enough of what Tarshea was saying to refute her big fat lie.

Diane rushed over and swept the girls up in her arms. "Who are you?" she asked Tarshea. "And what are you doing with my girls?"

"I think I can explain," Esme told Diane, who looked only marginally less upset than when she'd arrived.

"I am an artist and I painted their faces," Tarshea explained. "This is entirely my fault. There's an ice cream place and kids' play area at the other end of the field. Maybe we could go there?"

"*¿Helado para los dos?*" Esme asked the twins without waiting for Steven and Diane to respond. "Ice cream?"

You could hear the twins' cheer all the way back in Los Angeles.

Ten minutes later, the twins were happily eating ice cream and playing on a merry-go-round with about a dozen Jamaican kids. They couldn't really understand one another, because the girls' English was still limited and the Jamaican children had very thick accents, but they were laughing and spinning around like crazy tops just the same.

Esme and Tarshea sat directly across from Steven and Diane at a small redwood picnic table. The Goldhagens were in a dark mood as Tarshea tried to defend Esme.

"I asked Esme to get something out of one of my make-up bags," Tarshea invented. "Then a friend of mine came over and distracted me. I called to Esme to follow me through the crowd, but I forgot that I was speaking in patois and she couldn't understand me. So you see, it really is my fault entirely."

"But Esme should have been watching them the whole time," Diane pointed out to Steven. "That's her job."

Esme didn't know what to say. Mostly, she was grateful to Tarshea for covering for her, because Diane was right. It was Esme's job to watch the children, and she shouldn't have taken her eyes off them.

Steven sighed and turned to his wife. "You know, Diane, there was no harm done. We've got our girls. They look happy. And I think Esme's done a hell of a job here, especially with Peter and Erin's kids. They've been murder on her. Tell me *you* wanted to take care of them. Look at Esme. She's exhausted!"

Thank you, God.

"Why did you make the announcment in Spanish?" Diane asked sharply. "What were you afraid of, Esme?"

Shit. "I didn't want everyone to know the girls were missing," Esme improvised. "I thought someone bad might find them and decide to hold them for ransom. Or something."

"I'd say that was pretty damn smart." Steven nodded admiringly, and then looked at Tarshea. "I want to thank you, too. For helping out. But also for taking responsibility for what you did. You don't know us. But you did it anyway."

Esme turned to Tarshea. "I can't thank you enough."

Hint-hint. Esme had only twenty dollars in her pocket. She could give it to Tarshea, sure. But Steven Goldhagen could peel ten—hell, a *hundred*—times that off his money wad and never know it was missing.

Esme looked over at the girls. Weston was rubbing her eyes—a sure sign that she was tired. And why shouldn't she be tired? It had been a huge day, and they still had the big drive across the island back to Northern Look.

Diane noticed too. "Steven, I think the girls have had enough. It's probably time to drive back."

"Definitely." Steven stood up. So did Diane, Esme, and Tarshea.

Damn. No reward. But maybe there's something I can do.

"I couldn't have found the girls without Tarshea," Esme said quickly. "She . . . got the band to stop playing so I could get up there."

Steven smiled. "A go-getter. Maybe you have a future in Hollywood."

Esme jumped on the comment, though not necessarily in

the way that Steven was thinking. "I totally agree with you," she told him. "Which is why I was wondering if maybe you've got some friends who might need a nanny like Tarshea? Someone really caring and responsible, who cared about Easton and Weston when she didn't even have to."

Steven fixed his eyes on Tarshea. "What I would ask is, is Tarshea interested?"

Tarshea nodded emphatically. "I could provide excellent references, sir. But what I really want to do is go to art school in America."

"Well then." Steven took out a business card, gave it to her, and then dug around for a pen. "What's your address? Phone number?"

Tarshea's face fell. "We have an address, but I don't trust the mail to get there. We don't have a telephone. We cannot afford a telephone."

"No phone?" Diane was incredulous. "How do you *communicate*?"

"We manage," Tarshea told her, a little embarrassed. "It's different here in Jamaica."

"Do you have someone else who the Goldhagens can contact?" Esme urged.

"How about . . . my minister?" Tarshea suggested. "He has a phone. I'll give you the number." She took the pen and quickly jotted some information. "Thank you," Tarshea told Steven. "I appreciate it very much."

Esme looked at her closely. She was grateful that the Goldhagens had offered to help, but there was also . . . what was the emotion in her eyes? Skepticism. Like, not wanting to be disappointed if these Americans went back to their country and never gave another thought to Tarshea the artist.

"They'll be in touch," Esme declared. This kind girl had saved her ass; the least she could do was to try and return the favor.

"Dang!" Lydia exclaimed as she admired Kiley's new digs—a bungalow guesthouse beside the hillside mansion that belonged to Dirk and Beth Paulson and their daughter, Grace. Kiley had called Lydia as soon as she'd settled into her new home; after all, Lydia lived only two doors away.

"You, Kiley McCann, have hit the jackpot. Wanna trade jobs?"

As she stood in the center of her guesthouse, Kiley indeed felt as though she'd hit the jackpot. The place was amazing, even nicer than the guesthouse she'd had at Platinum's. There were not one, not two, but three full bedrooms. The master bedroom was on the ground floor; it was paneled in oak, and had an oak king-sized bed, and featured an enormous picture window that looked out onto a formal garden with a koi fish-pond and a gazebo that Beth had explained was used only for meditation. Upstairs were two other bedrooms, half the size of hers, each decorated in a different theme. One was Japanese, with a futon on the floor, Japanese art on the walls, and a single perfect rose in a clear glass bud vase. The other was a bit odd, decorated like a cheap motel room—colorless rug, basic nature-themed prints on the walls, two matching no-name lamps on nightstands, and a tiny dresser. There was an upstairs bathroom with shower, while the downstairs bathroom—Kiley's main one—was black marble and enormous, and featured a Jacuzzi big enough to hold six adults comfortably. The golden Moen fixtures probably cost more than a mortgage payment back in La Crosse.

It was two hours or so after Kiley's unpleasant ending to her experience with Evelyn Bowers. Of course, it wasn't entirely over—she realized that she would probably run into Evelyn and her charming children at the country club.

The Paulsons had been extremely nice and extremely thoughtful—just as they'd been at the country club, but even more so. They said they would treat Kiley like an adult, and treat Kiley's guesthouse as though it belonged to her. If she wanted to have friends there—even to stay over, Beth said without any embarrassment—that was up to Kiley. Of course, it couldn't interfere with her work. The only other thing that she needed to be aware of was that the family home gym was attached to the guesthouse. Both Dirk and Beth were pretty fanatical about staying in shape.

Grace had shown Kiley her room, which turned out to be an homage to the world's greatest art museums. There were posters from the Louvre, the new Museum of Modern Art in New York City, the Prado in Madrid, the Hermitage in St. Petersburg, plus some others that Kiley didn't recognize. Grace had explained her love of sculpture, and there were reproductions of works by Michelangelo and Giacometti, plus an original Alexander Calder mobile that hung from the ceiling above Grace's single bed. Grace had explained that her parents were just finishing an art studio for her at the far end of the property and that she couldn't wait for it to be done.

Kiley was so excited when she left the big house that she'd immediately called Lydia—it was so amazing that she was going to live just houses away from one of her two best friends. Lydia somehow managed to beg a half hour off; the Paulsons lived close enough for her to walk over.

"As soon as I was coming right over, the Paulsons stocked the fridge," Kiley told Lydia. "Sort of a welcome-to-our-house thing. You want anything?"

Lydia shook her head. "Nah. I just had a double wheatgrass-and-tofu milk shake, of which I had to drink the whole thing under the watchful eye of the Merry Matron of Moscow. Have you ever tasted that shit? I mean, seriously, it tastes like ass."

Kiley laughed. Her cell phone rang and she trotted into the living room where she'd left it. "Hello?"

"Kiley. It's Tom."

Kiley's legs felt weak. "Hi."

"How are you?"

"Okay." Lydia wandered in and watched Kiley, leaning against the wall. Kiley mouthed that it was Tom.

"So, look, I know I haven't called you," Tom went on. "I just—I figured you didn't want me to. I mean, you made it pretty clear you want to cool things with me. So if it's friendship you want, then—"

"Wait, wait," Kiley interrupted. "I didn't say I wanted to be *friends*!" Across the room, Lydia rolled her eyes.

"You kind of did," Tom pointed out. "Not in so many words, maybe, but—"

"No, I . . ." It was now or never. "The truth is, I got scared. That's all. I definitely want more from you than friendship. I figured you never wanted to see me again—"

Tom laughed. "Man, we are two idiots, huh?"

"Well, that's a big yes on my end," Kiley replied giddily.

"So when can I see you?"

His low, throaty voice sent shivers down her spine. Even though she'd just arrived at the Paulsons', she reminded herself that they'd insisted she wouldn't start working until the next afternoon. She was absolutely free for the evening. And the morning.

She told him to come over and gave him her new address. When she hung up the phone, she jumped up and hugged Lydia as hard as she could. "He's coming over!"

"*Sex with a Supermodel* is back on?" Lydia queried.

"Yes," Kiley affirmed. "Screw Marym. Tom Chappelle is mine!"

"That's the spirit!" Lydia glanced at her watch. "I've been here for exactly ten minutes."

"So?" Kiley bounced onto the buttery soft gray Italian leather couch, buoyant with happiness.

"So it took me six to get here, walking downhill. I have a half hour for a break. I suck at math, but I think that leaves me fourteen minutes to slog back to the gulag."

"Well, that sucks." Kiley rose and hugged her friend. "Thanks for coming over to see my new digs."

"You're welcome, even if I am terminally jealous. I'll see you at the club tomorrow?"

"I don't know yet. I have to find out what they want me to do."

"I hope Esme gets back soon," Lydia moaned. "I really need someone to bitch with and you're way too happy."

They said their goodbyes and Lydia departed, after which Kiley flew around the guesthouse getting ready for Tom. Did she have time to shower? She couldn't risk it. She wet an embroidered washcloth that she found in a stack on the white

wicker shelf in the bathroom and gave herself a quick once-over. What to wear with a boy who was about to undress you? She decided on her white Gap V-neck tee that hinted at the faintest of cleavage, and her usual jeans. This was her, and, she finally believed, it was her whom Tom wanted. But . . . a little perfume couldn't hurt. She fished the sample vial of Clinique Happy she'd found in her bathroom at Evelyn's out of her purse and applied some to the pulse points on her wrists and neck. Happy indeed.

Fifteen minutes later, he was knocking on the front door. As soon as he walked in, she was in his arms, his lips on hers. "Kiley," he whispered.

"I'm so glad you're here," she whispered back. He wore a Ben Sherman striped polo and darkly tinted jeans, and looked incredibly hot. This was it. This was finally, finally it. Boldly, she led him into her bedroom.

He sat on the edge of her pillow-strewn bed. "I don't know. I think you'd better call your mother first."

What? "You've got to be kidding. Do you want her to call out the National Guard?"

Tom laughed, pulled Kiley down onto the bed, and tickled her. "To tell her that you're not working for Evelyn Bowers anymore."

She bopped him with a down-pillow. "Oh, you think you're soooo funny."

"So do you."

Then his lips were on hers again, and she couldn't think of anything except him.

22

Lydia ran her hand over the hood of Luis's new Toyota Spyder, which was parked on the street in front of his rented house, a cute Craftsman-style bungalow on Twenty-third Avenue in Santa Monica. On the ride back to his place after he had picked her up at the moms' house, Luis had explained that he shared this house with another golf pro, a guy named Jeff who taught at the Riviera Country Club.

"Great car," she murmured. "Nice engine. You gonna let me take her for a drive?"

Luis smiled. "I have something else in mind. Follow me."

"If you think we're going to have sex, think again," Lydia told him, but followed him up the short driveway to the detached garage just to the north of the house. "I only have sex when I want to have sex, and bribes don't work."

He looked at her curiously. "How often do you want to?"

"Well, actually, to date I've had sex zero times," she admitted in her usual forthright manner, as she noticed a For Sale sign on the small front lawn. "But that is beside the point. Hey, how much are they asking for this place?"

The home was no great shakes—just a little bigger than her guesthouse at the moms', and not in particularly good condition either. The white paint was peeling, the asphalt driveway was cracked and worn, and as they approached the garage, Lydia saw that the wooden garage door was rotting badly.

"Three bedrooms, one bathroom," Luis recited. "Sixteen hundred square feet. Built in 1955. Needs a new furnace. Only three of the burners work on the stove, and the oven not at all. The backyard floods when it rains, and you can't run the microwave and an iron at the same time or else the fuses blow out."

"So how much?" Lydia asked again as Luis lifted up the garage door. It creaked uneasily on its track as he did. "A hundred fifty thousand?"

"Try a million two." Luis smiled thinly. "Kind of out of my price range. Which is why I'm thinking about moving to south Florida."

"That's a lot of money," Lydia commented when the garage door was up.

Luis flipped on a light. There, parked in the garage, was a gorgeous orange two-seater sports car. It had an open cockpit, just two doors, a metal luggage rack of some kind on the trunk, wheels with chrome hubs, and sparkling chrome front and rear bumpers.

"Nineteen seventy-five Triumph Spitfire," Luis proclaimed.

"Fifteen-hundred-cc engine, wood-grain dashboard, hundred and twelve thousand miles on it. Four-speed manual transmission. Top speed of a hundred and twenty."

"Is this yours?" Lydia breathed, picturing herself behind the wheel of this beauty, tooling down Sunset Boulevard at twilight, waving to the cute guys she passed.

"Yup. It needs some work. I don't think the clutch will last more than another few thousand miles. Ditto the tires. Take a look."

Lydia looked, though what she knew about automobile tires was negligible.

"See?" Luis pointed. "Tread's almost gone. But you can take it home if you want it. It runs."

What?

Something in her eyes must have said yes, because a set of car keys was soaring through the air toward her, courtesy of an easy toss from Luis. She reached up and caught them.

Well. Here was a set of wheels, handed to her on a silver platter. She didn't have to pay for them either. "You're sure you don't expect sexual favors in return?"

Luis laughed. "Only if you insist. It's on loan for as long as you need it. Just make sure it comes back to me in one piece. Driveable. I'm going to sell it eventually."

Okay, so the boy was funny. She wasn't that concerned about how the Spitfire would require significant repairs in a month or two, or how she would explain the acquisition of this vehicle to Billy. It didn't matter that she didn't officially have a driver's license, or that she barely knew the guy who was lending her the car. What mattered was that she now had a way to get from point A to point B—almost the price of admission to Los Angeles.

She couldn't wait to see how shocked Anya would be. That would be fun.

Uh-oh. There was one problem.

"Umm . . . this car has a standard transmission?" Lydia asked.

"Yup."

"I . . . can't say I've ever driven one before." She didn't add the more salient detail, that she'd spent exactly two hours behind any kind of wheel at all. She might be outspoken, but she chose her spots. "Is it fun?"

Luis laughed. "It is. Start 'er up. I'll show you how it's done. You definitely look like you can handle a stick."

Oh yeah.

As it turned out, Lydia could very well handle it. Luis took her back to the parking lot at Santa Monica College, which was only a mile or so from his house. There, he gave her the world's quickest lesson on how to handle a clutch and the gearshift. It took Lydia only about fifteen minutes to figure out which foot should go on which pedal. Though she stalled out a few times, and Luis warned her about the challenges of starting a stickshift car from a dead stop while going uphill, he quickly decided that she was competent enough to take the Spitfire out on the Pacific Coast Highway.

Of course, Lydia didn't bother to volunteer that she could measure the time that she'd been driving in hours instead of in days, and that she merely had a learner's permit. It was a don't-ask, don't-tell policy. Luis didn't ask, and Lydia didn't tell.

The Pacific Coast Highway was clear; it was a perfect moonlit evening. With Luis urging her on, Lydia raced through the gears as they sped north through Santa Monica and Malibu. It was only when Lydia reached eighty-five miles an hour on a straight-away that Luis suggested she use some caution.

"Not that I'm opposed to driving fast," he told her. "It's just that this is a famous speed trap."

They stopped for a drink at a bar that Luis knew in Malibu—the bartender was only too happy to spike Lydia's Coke with a healthy shot of vodka—where they toasted Lydia's newfound prowess behind the wheel. Luis drank only non-fortified orange juice, so Lydia felt free enough to have another spiked Coke, and then another. They danced to the tunes wailing from the jukebox, Lydia snaking her arms around his neck sexily as they did.

There were various herbal highs available in the Amazon, and Lydia had tried most of them. But alcohol was new to her. She had no idea how much would make her tipsy, drunk, or utterly smashed. And frankly, she didn't feel like thinking about it because she was having way too much fun.

"Ready to take me for a ride, Mr. Pro?" Lydia whispered. Because what the hell. It was only flirting. And it wasn't as if she was married. It also wasn't as if flirting with Billy got her anywhere.

"Definitely," Luis told her.

The drive back to Santa Monica took only about twenty minutes, Luis pointedly racing through the speed trap on the PCH, to Lydia's delight. To celebrate, she whipped off her heather gray cutoff sweatshirt, whirled it overhead, and then flung it into the night. The wind caught it and it took off behind them for parts unknown, leaving her clad only in her recently acquired secondhand Rock & Republic jeans (which she cinched with a gray ribbon since they were far too large) and a silvery Cosabella bra shot through with inky embroidery. It was one she had taken from her aunt's stash days before, but you couldn't very well return worn underwear.

"I've had that sweatshirt since I was thirteen," Lydia chortled. She realized that she was more than a little bit toasted, but she was having such a great time that she didn't really care.

Luis eyed Lydia's flimsily covered breasts with appreciation. "You look better without it."

She leaned against him, her head swimming. "You say the sweetest things."

Luis draped an arm casually around the back of Lydia's seat. Then Yellowcard's "Ocean Avenue" came on the CD player, and Luis turned it up loud enough that it blasted through the Triumph's open cockpit.

"You know this song?" Luis shouted.

"No way! I lived in the rain forest for eight years! No radio, no nothing!" she screamed into the wind.

"For real? Cool!"

"No, *hot*!" Lydia joked, and decided she was perhaps the funniest person she knew. She turned to Luis. Or rather, both Luises. Huh. Doubles. That was definitely an alcohol thing. How much had she ended up drinking, anyway? A lot. *A lot* a lot.

Whatever. She was having too much fun to worry about it, zooming down the highway with a cute boy, rock and roll blaring on the sound system and the Pacific Ocean just yards away. This was what she had dreamed of in Amazonia when she'd thought about coming to California and being a nanny. The only things missing were five or six credit cards in a mink-pelted

Coach hobo bag over her shoulder. Even that would be remedied soon enough, she decided. She was cute, smart, and unstoppable.

If there were any other traits necessary to thrive in Hollywood, she didn't know what they were.

"Tom," Kiley sighed.

"Kiley."

Kiley sighed again. It was going to be perfect this time. The stars had finally lined up the way they were supposed to for her. Now, they were together in her bed, in her darkened bedroom, in her guesthouse, at her new home in Beverly Hills, on the property of people who were shaping up to be the best employers any nanny could ask for.

Of course, she hadn't called her mother, because neither she nor Tom wanted to stop what they were doing. And yet, even after all the buildup, Tom insisted on going slowly. She was still in her white bikini panties and her T-shirt was still firmly over her bra; Tom was giving Kiley a back rub with almond lotion that was part of a welcome basket of toiletries she had found in the master bath. The back rub seemed to go on for an hour; it was so relaxing that Kiley felt like purring. Then he got up and found some L'Occitane lavender candles, which he lit and placed around Kiley's bedroom. He flipped through the radio stations, finally settling on some classical music.

Tom kissed her. It was heavenly. She got on her knees and tugged his T-shirt over his head, then ran her fingers down his chiseled abs. What had she been so nervous about? This was fantastic. She wound her arms around his neck and kissed him. His hands traveled under her T-shirt and up her back, still slick and almond-scented from his massage. She pulled the T-shirt over her head and felt his large fingers unhooking the back of her cottony bra.

Whap-whap. Whap-whap.

The sounds were coming from the home gym next door.

"What the hell was that?" Tom leaned on one elbow, listening intently.

Whap-whap. Whap-whap.

"I have no idea," Kiley replied, brushing back the hair that had fallen onto her face.

Whap-whap. Whap-whap.

The noise continued, loud and rhythmic.

"What's back there?" Tom asked.

"Their gym," Kiley reported. "Beth and Dirk told me they like to work out. Maybe they wait until Grace is asleep."

She checked the clock on her nightstand. Eleven o'clock. Surely Grace was asleep. Yes, that had to be it.

The commotion from the gym got louder. Now, faint rock and roll was trickling through the wall, along with the rhythmic thumping. It certainly interfered with the mellow ambiance of the flickering lights and sensuous classical music.

Well, they didn't have to let it ruin their evening, Kiley decided. She leaned forward and kissed Tom. Everything was going great again, when whoever was working out next door turned up the AC/DC. The vase on the dresser actually started to vibrate.

"Jeez," Tom groused. "They could have a little consideration."

"Oh, come on," Kiley said playfully. "How long can their workout be?"

"I don't—"

191

The wall behind the headboard of Kiley's bed actually started shaking. Hard. Then they heard the sounds of people cheering.

Cheering?

"How many people could possibly be in there?" Kiley wondered aloud.

Tom got to his feet and started scrounging around for his clothes.

"Where are you going?" Kiley asked.

"To check it out." He slipped his Calvin Klein—of course—jeans on. Kiley decided to go with him. She wiggled into her jeans and pulled her T-shirt back on. Then the two of them, barefoot in the warm evening, picked their way around the guesthouse in the dark toward the home gym in the back. It wasn't so hard to see, because every light in that gym was blazing, illuminating the stone path that led there from Kiley's front door. There was an auditory trail to follow too, because loud classic rock and roll—Kiley now recognized the Rolling Stones—blared through windows that she hoped were open. Otherwise, the volume inside the gym had to be earsplitting.

They reached the first exterior window of the home gym, a structure nearly as big as Kiley's guesthouse but built all on one floor. The window was indeed wide open. They peered inside.

Kiley's jaw dropped. Dirk and Beth were indeed "working out"—right up against the gym wall that was also the wall behind Kiley's bedroom. So were ten or fifteen other naked couples, in various combinations of men, women, and gym equipment used in ways that Kiley never had even *imagined.* Everyone was so preoccupied that no one noticed Kiley and Tom gaping at the window.

"Holy shit," Kiley gasped.

Tom cracked up. "This gives a whole new meaning to exercise."

"Shhh!" she warned. "They'll hear us." That was all Kiley could manage. Her gaze was fixed on her employers, unable to believe both what they were doing and how well they were doing it. Not that Kiley had ever seen *anybody* do it before. Just at that moment, Beth's eyes sprang open . . . and looked right at her and Tom. Kiley felt like a deer caught in someone's headlights. She just stood there in utter shock and embarrassment.

What happened next was even more shocking. Beth smiled at Kiley. Then she made the same crooking gesture with her finger that she'd made that afternoon in the country club's breezeway: the one that meant "Come over here."

Come over here? As in: Join the party? Was the woman demented? Most likely so. She had to realize that Kiley would hear her sexcapades. Was that part of the fun? How many nannies had she done this with? How many had taken her up on the offer?

Kiley turned to Tom. "Can we get out of here? Please?"

"Absolutely." He took her hand and led the way back to her brand-new-about-to-be-former guesthouse. "No need for a formal resignation. Consider yourself gone."

23

"Shhh," Luis cautioned. "Keep it down. People are sleeping."

"But we're not!" Lydia chortled exuberantly. "And if they wake up, they can come out here with us. You know what I want? Champagne! I need some champagne! Some fizzy lifting drinks!"

"Well then, I'd say you're in luck." Luis reached down and lifted the bottle of five-buck champagne he'd bought at the Ralph's supermarket at the corner of Sunset Boulevard and the Pacific Coast Highway, on their way back from Malibu. "Cook's. The beer of bubbly."

Lydia laughed so hard at this that tears leaked out the corners of her eyes. It was after midnight; they'd just returned from their drive up the coast. But Lydia wasn't ready to go home. What she wanted to do was go swimming the way she always swam in Amazonia. That is, sans swimsuit. Luis said he had just the thing: his next-door neighbors' pool. They were out of town, so there'd be no Peeping Toms—or Samanthas, Stevens, Debbies, or Moniques.

Luis twisted the cork out of the bottle—no satisfying pop, but what could you expect for five bucks?—took a serious swig, and handed the bottle to Lydia. She was standing at the edge of the pool in her underwear, barely illuminated by the underwater red and white lights.

"A toast to the Amazonian gods of water," she pronounced, upending the bottle and letting a steady stream flow into the pool. Then she lifted the bottle high and poured the same stream into her mouth.

"To the gods," Luis pronounced.

"Okay, I'm ready. If you are."

Luis quickly stripped off his clothes until he too was at the edge of the pool, wearing nothing but boxers.

"Good enough for me!" Lydia pulled her bra over her head and stepped out of her panties, then made a clumsy dive into the water. She came up grinning, to watch Luis jump in near her.

"Jeez, that's cold!" he exclaimed.

"You haven't had enough to drink," she scolded.

The pool felt great. She splashed around in it for a while, dunking herself down to the bottom and trying to hold herself there. That thought made her think of the sea, which made her think of Kiley, which made her think of what Kiley was doing right that instant. Probably having wild sex with Tom. She popped up to the surface, looked around for Luis, and saw him treading water by the diving board.

"I've got another great idea," she declared. "Let's go to your place."

"I thought you had a boyfriend," Luis said.

"I do. I think." Lydia giggled drunkenly as she sat up on Luis's bed and took another big swallow of the champagne, the bath towel that he'd given her wrapped around her body. He was next to her, back in his blue boxers, having switched from Cook's to Coors.

Her boyfriend. Billy. Right. She really, really, really liked Billy. But they had never said anything to each other about an "exclusive" relationship. In fact, they couldn't even see each other all that often due to their schedules. Oh sure, Billy said he wanted them to get to know each other before they . . . *got to know each other,* but in the back of Lydia's mind there was always a nagging voice asking how he could resist her. The maddening thing was, there was no good reason *to* resist her. She was hot, and Luis knew it even if Billy didn't.

The room was very dark; Luis had switched on just a dim night-light when they'd come in. She vaguely remembered him carrying her inside from the pool while she sang a song her mom used to sing to her when she was still the little rich southern princess back in Houston: *"I see the moon and the moon sees me and the moon sees somebody I want to see!"*

He'd shushed her, laughing as he did it. That was so cute.

She threw her arms over her head, not noticing that one of her breasts was very close to popping out of her bra.

"I want to feel . . . everything!" she told Luis, loose-limbed and woozy.

"With your boyfriend?" Luis asked, his lips nuzzling into her neck. "Or if you can't be with the one you love, love the one you're with?"

Lydia found this comment hilarious. She threw her head back and laughed, which made Luis laugh too. Soon, the two of them were rolling around on his bed, peals of laughter booming around his room.

What did she want? Her mind didn't want to focus. But she knew this much, even in her very inebriated state: she was sick to death of being a virgin. Back in the land of the Amas, where teens got sexually active very early without the taboos and guilt that existed in America, her mom had given Lydia "the talk" when she was twelve years old. Lydia should not succumb to the sexual freedom of the Amas. Though she lived among them, it wasn't her culture. This seemed patently unfair to Lydia. It wasn't as if she could go to dances or movies or date the guy who lived down the block.

Lydia decided not to listen to her mother. The problem was, Ama guys didn't appeal to her. They were short, they had sticks through their cheeks, and no one had found a profitable way to sell them Rembrandt tooth polish. So Lydia had to be content with the photographs of Tom Welling, Jared Leto, and Orlando Bloom she stuck to the walls of her hut with mud, dreaming about the day a gorgeous boy would introduce her to the wonderful world of lust.

Luis kissed down her neck, then brought his lips to hers. He tasted like beer, but it felt wonderful. She kissed him back.

"So . . . can we forget the boyfriend?" Luis whispered in her ear.

"Kinda." Lydia didn't know what "kinda" meant, but she felt much too good to stop and analyze it. All she wanted was to live in the moment; was that too much to ask? Did everything have to be so damn complicated?

No, she decided. It did not. Everything Luis was doing felt fantastic. He was here and she was here and there was no reason for her to tell him to stop.

So she didn't.

24

The next morning, Esme awoke in her own bed at the Gold-hagens' guesthouse, and looked around her room uncertainly. It had been a very long night; the Goldhagens' private jet had landed at the Van Nuys airport well after midnight, even with the three-hour time difference between Jamaica and Los Ange-les. She glanced at her clock—9:30 a.m. Thank God the Gold-hagens had told her she didn't have to be up at the main house until eleven, because they wanted the twins to sleep as long as they could.

The decision to come back to L.A. had been sudden, even before their van had arrived late the previous afternoon at the Northern Look resort after the outing to the sugarcane-cutting competition. As soon as they got in range of a cell phone tower, Steven had checked his messages. There'd been one from his office, announcing that an important pitch meeting with ABC had had to be moved up. Steven had been approached to try to create a new half-hour soap that would air nightly—the programming chief at ABC was so anxious to hear the pitch that it had been set for the next day, Steven's vacation be damned. It had surprised Esme that a man as powerful and famous as Steven Goldhagen didn't call the shots on when the meeting would take place.

Diane had been understanding; in fact, she had taken charge of making the last-minute travel arrangements and getting Steven's office to send over all the preliminary work that had been done on the soap, which Steven was tentatively calling *Generations*, after the three generations of a Norweigan family who settle in a fictitious town in Minnesota. Steven had told Esme all about the pitch a few days earlier, even asking her opinions about some of the characters. Odd, how sometimes the Goldhagens would converse with her as if she was a close friend, and other times she was an employee to be ordered around. Nicely ordered around, of course.

The helicopter had arrived at Northern Look three hours later; an hour after that, they were back on the private jet to Los Angeles. The Silversteins had elected to stay in Jamaica for a few more days, a decision that Esme had privately applauded. Enduring them for a long plane ride—in other words, close quarters in a confined space—would have been torture.

Esme got up, took a quick shower, and made herself some coffee, happy to have a morning to herself. She had come to love living in this little house, so lovely and calm, so unlike her old life. She remembered how hard it had been for her to fall asleep those first few nights. She was used to the noise and music and smells of the barrio. But here it was so quiet. She curled up on the couch in her living room, enjoying the scent from the orange blossoms that wafted through the open window. Now she was used to it. Now she loved it.

Love. Was part of loving this place her feelings for Jonathan? She took another sip of her coffee. She'd deliberately tried not to think of him when she was in Jamaica; in that way, the Silverstein boys from hell were a fortunate distraction. Yet she couldn't put off making a decision about him much longer. It wasn't fair to anyone. A person could not have one foot on either side of a fault line. But how could she possibly hurt Junior, dis him, by telling him that she'd chosen the rich gringo over him? She felt ashamed just thinking about the conversation.

"*Hola, niña.*"

"Mama!" She saw her mom outside her guesthouse, heading toward her front door. Esme met her at the doorstep and embraced her. They held the hug for a long time.

"Welcome home," her mother said in Spanish. "I understand you had quite a trip. Diane has been raving about you all morning, about how wonderful you were with all the children."

Well. That was unexpected news. Evidently the little detail about Esme having actually *lost the girls* was not foremost on Diane's mind.

"Come in for a minute," Esme urged. She adored her mother, and since she'd started to work at the Goldhagens' she felt as though she never got to spend enough time with her, even though they were both working for the same employer. "I've made coffee."

"I can stay for a little while," Estella Castaneda agreed. "Your father and I started very early this morning. I could use a break."

Mrs. Castaneda followed her daughter through the guest-house into the kitchen, where Esme poured her a mug of steaming Colombian coffee, black with one sugar, just the way she liked it. When her mom sat, put her feet up at Esme's urging, and then sighed with contentment at the first sip, Esme felt great. Back in her parents' small bungalow in Echo Park, she'd always been the first one to wake up and make the coffee. Watching her mom, with both hands around her mug, steam rising gently to her chin, made Esme a little bit homesick.

"What are you thinking, my daughter?" Estella asked. "You look so serious."

"I miss you and Papa," Esme confessed. "I never get to see you."

"We miss you, too, *niña*. But we are so happy that you are going to have a wonderful future."

Esme sighed. The Goldhagens had promised that if things worked out, Esme could go to Beverly Hills High for her senior year and nanny only part-time. They'd even talked about paying for her to go to UCLA. It was a fantastic, amazing, once-in-a-lifetime opportunity, but it all seemed so abstract. In the present, all she knew was that she missed her family.

"I'm not so sure I like it," Esme confessed.

"This is why back in Mexico, so many people never leave their village. Or they go to Mexico City or Guadalajara to look for work, but still come home. They would rather be poor and have their family than earn money and be all alone. But you, my daughter . . ." She leaned forward and gently took Esme's chin in her hand. "You are so smart, Esme. You will be the first person in our family to attend college. That is a blessing."

Something in her mother's voice made her think of Tarshea, the young artist she'd met in Jamaica. Tarshea came from a poor place, but wanted nothing more than to follow her dream of studying art in a real art school. She'd have to leave her family behind to do it too.

"Maybe," Esme allowed. "But I still would like it if we spent more time together as a family. You and me and Papa. I never see him, either."

Estella smiled. "He's repairing the water fountain out by the tennis court. If you want to say hello."

Esme shook her head. "I didn't mean like that. Not here, where we're the workers."

"Well, maybe you could come home on the weekend instead of going out with your friends here," Estella said pointedly.

Her mother was right. Echo Park might have been in another economic universe, but it was only ten miles from Bel Air. The truth was, Esme had been wanting to spend her weekends with Jonathan, or hang out with Lydia and Kiley. If only she could clone herself.

She resolved to go home that weekend—to make *carne mexicana y arroz con rajitas y elote* with her father, drink *horchata* with Jorge, maybe even go dancing with some of her old girlfriends.

Then she realized that she had left Junior out of this plan. It made her feel so conflicted that she wanted to change the subject. "So, did you just stop by to say hello?"

"Yes and no."

"What's the no?"

"Junior stopped over when you were in Jamaica. He's doing a lot better."

Esme's stomach clenched, all the more so considering what she'd just been thinking about. "That's good." She tried to sound upbeat.

"Perhaps. I don't know. He told me that he wants to see you. And he wants to see Jonathan. At the same time."

"Well, there goes my dream job," Kiley told Tom. They were eating breakfast at the outdoor portion of Cafe Med, a small restaurant on the north side of Sunset Boulevard just west of Tower Records. Tom had told her that Cafe Med was well known as a Eurotrash hangout—Eurotrash being rich young Europeans who had enough money to come to America and do nothing for long stretches of time. From the different languages being spoken by the good-looking couples and trios at the tables around them, Kiley decided that the reputation was well deserved. "It's beneath my minimum moral standards."

"Oh, I don't know," Tom teased, "you could have just waltzed in there last night and grabbed yourself a partner—"

"Very funny." Kiley swallowed a mouthful of her avocado-and-sweet-onion omelet. "I still can't believe that happened. Maybe everyone in this town really *is* insane."

Kiley couldn't help thinking it had barely been a week since she'd sat with Jorge at the restaurant in the Echo after having lost her job at Platinum's. Since then, she'd been through two more nanny gigs, each more disastrous than the one before. She was beginning to lose hope.

Last night, after Tom had helped her pack her things, they'd come back to his hotel suite. He'd understood that Kiley wasn't in the mood to continue what they'd started. After a sweet kiss goodnight, she'd slept alone in the second bedroom.

She put her fork down. "What am I going to do?"

Tom sipped his fresh-squeezed orange juice. "Damned if I know," he admitted. "Maybe you can go back to the country club and wait for someone else to poach you."

"Yeah, great, the next couple will probably sell me into slavery. That place is *dangerous*."

"I'm not sure you have much of a choice." Tom edged forward to let a tall, gorgeous girl get past him. Her straight blond hair fell nearly to her butt, a silvery contrast to her black Versace tank top emblazoned with the designer's Medusa logo—clearly she had on nothing underneath—a black pleated miniskirt studded with grommets, and silver and black Puma sneakers. It was a sleek combination of casual and couture that oozed cool. Instead of going by, she stopped and put both her hands seductively on Tom's shoulders.

"Tom Chappelle?" she asked in a thick Italian accent.

Tom twisted around, his face lighting up.

"Veronica!" Tom exclaimed. "I haven't seen you since—"

"Milan. In April," she reminded him.

"That was a great time," Tom recalled, then looked at Kiley. "Kiley, I want you to meet the one and only Veronica. Veronica, my friend Kiley."

"My pleasure." Veronica extended a perfect hand—long, thin fingers with long, thin nails.

"Good to meet you, Veronica," Kiley said, trying to sound chipper. What was up with Tom? Did he know every gorgeous model in the civilized world or did it only seem that way?

Veronica leaned over. Her blond hair brushed Tom's face as she kissed his cheek. "Call me, okay? *Ciao*." She disappeared down Sunset Boulevard, blond hair swinging.

How did models do that walk, Kiley wondered, where they put one foot directly in front of the other on each step, so that their butt shifted sexily from side to side? She'd once tried to copy it in the privacy of her bedroom back in La Crosse after watching *America's Next Top Model* with Nina. The experiment was hopeless. A) She had nearly tripped over her own feet, and B) she felt like a total ass.

She was about to take an actual bite of her omelet when Tom's words of introduction rang again in her ears.

My friend Kiley. That was what he'd said. Not *my girlfriend, Kiley.* Just *my friend Kiley.*

Wow, that made her feel like shit.

"What?" Tom asked.

"I didn't say anything."

"You just sighed like the weight of the world is on your shoulders."

"How about the weight of no job, no place to live, et cetera, et cetera."

Tom took a sip of his coffee. "You can live with me."

As what? Bestest friends? There was no point in having that conversation, because it wasn't an option, no matter what. Her mom still didn't know that she wasn't working for Evelyn Bowers. She had to find another nanny gig. But how?

"Okay, so say I do go back to the country club and stand in the breezeway," Kiley mused. "I must already be known as the girl who has lost three nanny gigs in about as many days. No one is going to want to—"

Her cell rang. She plucked it from her faux-leather purse from Target, praying it wasn't her mother. "Hello?"

"Is this Kiley McCann?" The voice was familiar; she'd heard it before. An adult woman. But she couldn't place it.

"That's me," Kiley told her.

"This is Tonika Johnson, City Department of Social Services," the voice told her. "We met a few nights ago at Platinum's home."

Tonika Johnson. Now Kiley remembered. She was the intense and businesslike social worker who had been at Platinum's mansion the night Platinum had been arrested and the children taken away by the department. Where they'd ended up when they were removed from the home, Kiley didn't know.

Why was this woman calling her now?

"Yes, of course I remember you," Kiley told Ms. Johnson. Tom was looking at her quizzically, but Kiley turned away so that he couldn't observe her face.

"I have some good news. Platinum's children are back in the house."

What?

"Oh my God, that's fantastic!" Kiley exclaimed. "Platinum's out of jail?"

"No, she's still in custody," the social worker reported. "And will be, for the foreseeable future. However, the children are back at home. We were able to locate Platinum's sister in San Diego. She and her husband were willing to come to Los Angeles and serve as guardians. Whenever possible, we prefer that solution to placing the children in shelters or with strangers."

"That's great news," Kiley said. She was so happy for the kids. She really did care about them. Sure, they were a handful. And they were spoiled, not to mention rife with weird phobias.

But basically, Serenity and Sid were regular kids who needed more structure and stability than they ever got from their mom.

"Thank you for calling to tell me," Kiley went on. "That was very thoughtful of you."

"Wait, Kiley. Don't hang up," the social worker implored. "There's more. I just got off the phone with Susan, Platinum's sister. She wanted to know if you would be available to be the children's nanny again."

25

It was lovely.

Lydia felt Billy curl his arms around her; his soft kisses on the back of her neck. The night before, she'd finally done the deed. Billy was gentle, considerate. There was no rush. It was all just so—

Her eyes snapped open; she took in her surroundings. She was in an unfamiliar bed in an unfamiliar bedroom. She saw a cheap brown dresser with white polo shirts and accompanying pants strewn atop it, a faded System of a Down poster taped to the wall with edges curling, and another of Tiger Woods punching the air after making a famous putt on some even more famous green.

Holy shit.

The night came roaring back to her. The car ride up to Malibu. The heavily fortified sodas. Throwing her favorite hoodie sweatshirt out into the night. The cheap champagne and the skinny-dipping and the . . .

Shit, shit, shit.

She heard snoring behind her and looked over her shoulder. Luis. She didn't even know Luis. Only now she *knew* Luis.

"Goddamn."

"Huh?" Luis groggily opened his eyes, focused on Lydia, and smiled. "Hey, you."

"Hey." Lydia peered at the old-fashioned windup clock on the nightstand. Eight-forty-three. Eight forty-three? She was so screwed! Anya had taken Martina and Jimmy up to Montecito for an overnight at the American home of some famous Russian tennis star, but would be back by nine-thirty so that the kids could continue their normal routine. Swimming lessons. Computer training. Russian lessons. An educational trip to the La Brea tar pits. Not to mention Martina's stadium-stairs run.

She jumped out of bed and started rooting around for her clothes, trying to ignore the blood rushing to her pounding head. The floor was a mess—she could barely see the carpet under the discarded warm-up suits, empty grease-stained pizza boxes, and CD cases. Where the hell was her stuff?

"What are you doing?" Luis asked languidly. "Come on back here."

"I've got to go," Lydia muttered. She found her jeans and pulled them on. "Gotta work."

"Me too." Luis sat back on his elbows. "You were amazing."

Yeah, yeah, yeah. Where were her silver T-strap heels? She didn't chuck them out of the car too, did she?

"I won't tell your boyfriend, you know. My lips are sealed."

"You don't even know my boyfriend," Lydia reminded him. She found the sandals under the bed, tangled up with a pair of tighty-whities. Ugh. On they went; then she dug in her pocket for the keys to the Triumph.

"I'm still good on the car?"

"Yeah," he told her as she searched for her bra and shirt—neither of which she could find. "Why not?"

"Thanks. Hope you don't mind if I borrow one of your shirts," she said, going to an open drawer and extracting a T-shirt advertising some brand of golf balls.

Luis nodded sleepily. "I'll call you."

"How about if I call you," Lydia suggested, pulling the T-shirt over her head. Ouch. The contact of cotton on scalp exacerbated what was turning into a splitting headache. "Hate to whatever and run, but . . . got to. Bye."

That was the best she could manage, considering how she had to get her ass back to work. Remember how to drive a stick shift. Figure out how to get one of those morning-after pills she'd read about in *Glamour,* because she'd been too toasted to even think about a condom and she didn't seem to recall Luis magically pulling one out, either.

Of course, there were a lot of details she didn't recall. How could she have been so stupid? It wasn't that she had anything against sex for the sake of sex. If two people mutually wanted to bang each other's brains out hanging upside down from the rain forest canopy, more power to 'em.

The problem in this case was that one of those people had a boyfriend; a boyfriend she really, truly cared about. Which gave her one more huge thing to figure out: what to tell Billy.

Tom leaned out the driver's-side window toward the intercom at the closed security gate at Platinum's estate in Bel Air. "It's Tom Chappelle. I've got Kiley McCann with me," he said, after being asked to identify himself.

The male voice that came back was staticky, but clear in its imperious tone. "The gate will open. Please discharge your passenger and back away from gate. I will be monitoring on closed-circuit television. You have three minutes to accomplish this task. Thank you."

"But . . . she has luggage!"

"Miss McCann can leave it inside the gate at the bottom of the hill; the children will come down later to retrieve it. Thank you."

"But—"

There was no time for but. The intercom cut off, and the mechanical gate began to open.

"Weird," Tom commented. "I always used to drive up before."

"Most of the time, Platinum just left the gate open," Kiley recalled. "But that was because she was so wasted she couldn't remember to close it."

Tom pulled his truck through and took out Kiley's battered suitcase and canvas tote; all she had. "I feel ridiculous leaving you here like this." He frowned.

"I'm fine," Kiley assured him, though she could hear the strain in her own voice.

He gave her a quizzical look. "You okay?"

She felt like saying: *Are you asking your girlfriend, the one you were about to have sex with last night, or are you asking* your friend Kiley? The way Tom had introduced her to Veronica still stung.

Instead, she replied, "Yeah, sure," as breezily as possible. Even if she did find the nerve, now was not the time to broach the "my friend Kiley" thing. "I'll call you later and tell you how it's going."

"Okay." He pulled her into his arms. Evidently her resistance was palpable, because he held her at arm's length so that he could look into her eyes. "There's something wrong. I want to know what it is."

Maybe she was making something out of nothing. Maybe it would have sounded lame for him to have introduced her as his girlfriend. Kiley didn't know anymore. So once more she insisted that everything was fine, and fixed a smile on her face to prove it.

"Okay." Tom started back toward the truck.

Kiley was about to let it go at that—maybe she would tell him later, maybe she wouldn't. Then she heard herself calling to him—she just couldn't stop herself.

"Tom!"

He turned.

"If all I am is 'your friend Kiley,' that's how I'm going to treat you, too. Like my friend Tom. I don't go to bed with my friend Tom."

He hesitated, trying to figure out what Kiley meant. Then it seemed to dawn on him. "Wait. Is this about what I said at breakfast, when I introduced you to Veronica?"

Kiley nodded.

"But . . . I didn't mean anything by that!"

There was a note of desperation in Tom's voice that Kiley found strangely satisfying. "You said what you said, Tom," she pointed out.

He raised his palms skyward. "I wasn't thinking. . . . Obviously you're much more to me. Don't you think you might be overreacting a little?"

"Maybe." She took a few steps backward, up the hill. "Maybe not. We'll talk later, okay?"

Without waiting for his response, she started the long walk up to Platinum's mansion, and managed to resist the temptation to turn around and see what Tom was doing until she was halfway up the hill. That was when she heard a girl's voice calling to her.

"Kiley! Kiley! You're back, you're back, you're back!"

Serenity came charging down the hill. She threw herself into Kiley's arms, snarled hair flying. Kiley found herself hugging her tight. "I missed you, sweetie," she told her.

"I told them I wouldn't take a shower until I was with you again," Serenity proudly reported, a telltale musty smell emanating from her body.

"Well, that's the first thing we'll do, then," Kiley assured her. "A shower. Or a bath. You choose."

Serenity hugged Kiley. Kiley was deeply touched. She'd never gotten that kind of affection during her previous stint as the children's nanny.

Hand in hand, they headed for the house. It occurred to Kiley that Serenity was dressed in a most unusual manner. Gone were her way-too-sexy-for-her-years, "I got it on Melrose Avenue, if you have to ask how much it is you can't afford it" outfits. Instead, Serenity had on a pair of new jeans with a *crease,* a blue and white Los Angeles Dodgers T-shirt, and Nikes. Interesting. Maybe the state social worker had taken away Serenity's other clothes. Still, it nearly made Kiley chuckle. Serenity could be forced into different clothes, but she couldn't be forced into the bathtub.

As they neared the house, Bruce and Sid came into view, trotting side by side down the driveway.

"The colonel expects you at the house in two minutes," Bruce warned, without stopping to say a proper hello. "We're on a four-minute deadline to get your bags, Kiley. Don't slow us down!"

Bruce was fourteen and Sid was nine, and Kiley had never seen either of them do a lick of exercise before. They were puffing hard as they ran down the hill to retrieve Kiley's bags.

"Who's the colonel?" Kiley asked Serenity.

"Did you see *Freddy vs. Jason*?" she asked. "He's both."

"So. You're Kiley McCann."

"Yes, sir." Within ten seconds of meeting Platinum's sister and her husband, Kiley had learned that the husband didn't respond to yes or no. It had to be "yes, sir" or "no, sir."

"At ease, Kiley," he barked. "Have a seat."

They were in the living room—the same white-on-white living room where the police had discovered Platinum's drugs on the coffee table—and where Serenity had found and smoked enough of Mendocino's finest to give herself a scary allergic reaction. Kiley took a seat on one of the couches; the kids' aunt and uncle were on the other. The uncle sat ramrod straight; his wife, Susan, was next to him, legs primly folded. He was tall, with close-cropped graying hair, green eyes, and a jutting chin, and wore dark trousers and a black button-down shirt with all the buttons buttoned. On his feet were the shiniest patent leather dress shoes Kiley had ever seen.

As for his wife, Kiley wouldn't have been able to pick her out in a crowd as Platinum's sister for all the salt in the Pacific. There was a passing resemblance in the high cheekbones and blue eyes, but this woman's blond hair had been set in a chin-length flip and then sprayed into submission. Where Platinum's garb was seriously rock and roll, Susan dressed as if her wardrobe had come from Dowdy Department Store. Her skirt was red and green tartan plaid and reached her calves; her blouse was crisp white cotton; and a cameo brooch glinted at her throat. Most impressively—or oddly, depending on one's point of view—she wore knee socks. Red knee socks. With squeaky-clean brown loafers.

All Kiley could think was: *This woman makes my mom seem fashionable.* And: *Susan might be the children's blood relative, but the colonel wears the pants in the family, literally and figuratively.*

That the kids had called their uncle the colonel was no accident. Their uncle, Richard M. Jones, was indeed a colonel. Or had been, in the United States Marine Corps, before he'd retired two years earlier. That he and Susan lived in San Diego was no accident, either. After a number of combat deployments that took them around the world, Colonel Jones finished out his Marine Corps career as one of the commanders at Camp Pendleton, just north of San Diego. His job was to turn raw recruits into formidable soldiers—he was the guy who taught drill instructors that it was better to be feared than loved.

"May I tell you what I think, Miss McCann?" the colonel boomed. Kiley suspected she was going to hear his opinion whether she wanted to or not. "I didn't want to come on this mission. I don't much care for my sister-in-law. Platinum has no values. No ethics. No pride. Are you following me so far?"

"Yes," Kiley said, nodding hastily. "Um, sir."

"But when that call came from Social Services—" Susan began.

"We knew it was our duty to come here," the colonel concluded. "I'm glad we did. It's a good thing our own children are in college and the military, and that I'm retired. It made me available, which is just what these three children need. Some structure, discipline, and tough love. They're still young; I suspect that there is still time to shape them up. I'm sure you agree, Miss McCann?"

What could she possibly say?

"Yes, sir."

"Excellent," he boomed. "Now, McCann, I have one question for you."

"Sir?" Kiley asked, feeling as if she was in a really bad war movie.

"Are you with me, or are you against me?"

"Umm . . ." Kiley hedged. There wasn't much choice. She needed the job, and it certainly was true that Platinum's kids needed structure for a change. Whether this drill colonel was the one to provide it remained to be seen.

"I'm with you, sir."

"Why don't you tell her what her pay will be, dear?" Susan asked.

"Same as with Platinum, not a penny more or less," he barked. "I'd call that fair, McCann. You?"

Jeez.

"Yes, sir," she replied.

"Excellent. Now, McCann, one more thing. We can't have two generals here. I suspect that the children are going to be looking to you for rescue, divide and conquer, all that." The colonel was on a roll. "So, Miss McCann, these are my terms: it's my way or the highway. Do we understand each other?"

"Yes, sir," Kiley said again. Clearly this was not a give-and-take kind of conversation.

He offered her a tight smile. "Now, about the uniform."

The colonel looked Kiley up and down, and Kiley suddenly got very self-conscious about her simple jeans and battered T-shirt combination.

"There will be a dress code for you when you are on duty. You will wear clean trousers, black, no denim, a shirt with a collar. White or pastel will be fine. I don't want the children having to wear anything that we would not require of ourselves. Do I need to have Susan take you to the PX for clothes?"

"Dear," Susan began. "There is no PX here. We're in Los Angeles."

"Of course, old habit," the colonel boomed. "The stores. The . . . mall." He said these words as if they were distasteful in his mouth.

"I don't own black trousers or white or pastel shirts with collars, sir," Kiley said.

He nodded and turned to his wife. "Understood. Take Kiley shopping. Let's give her a two-hundred-and-fifty-dollar clothing allowance. That should be sufficient. You understand the dress code, Kiley?"

"I do, sir."

The colonel stood up and stuck out his hand. Kiley shook. "Well then, welcome aboard."

"It's good to be back, sir," Kiley acknowledged, grinning a little at how official she sounded.

"Please go upstairs and tell the junior division to assemble down here in two minutes. For each minute they are late, they can expect two additional minutes of silence after dinner at the table. Dinner will be at eighteen hundred hours."

Whatever the hell that was.

"Yes, sir. I'll be right back."

Kiley's head was pounding as she bounded up the stairs. This guy really thought he was going to get all Platinum's kids at the dinner table at the same time? Kiley could scarcely remember a meal where the entire family had been together at the table. Usually, each kid drifted down, got something from Mrs. Cleveland, the chef, and then brought it back upstairs to their room to eat.

Things are definitely going to be different, Kiley thought. That, or the kids were going to mutiny. Either way, she didn't intend to go down with the ship.

26

"You don't think this is bordering on the melodramatic?" Jonathan asked Esme as they headed up Alvarado Street in Echo Park to meet Junior. It was twilight, and the busy street was teeming with people shopping, flirting, or just hanging out. Jonathan wore casual olive green cargo shorts and a black T-shirt with simple Reef flip-flops; Esme appreciated that he'd dressed so as not to stand out in her old neighborhood. Esme had followed suit in her low-slung black pants with a white men's tank, but was still conscious of the junkie who was nodding out against a streetlight, the spilled garbage from an overturned trash can on the corner, and the graffiti covering the bus stop that had no bench lest hookers or the homeless wanted to make themselves comfortable.

"I've known Junior a long time," Esme replied. "If he says he wants to see us together, it's respect for us to come."

"You don't think his homies are going to be there to kick my ass, huh?" Jonathan asked archly, clearly only half-joking.

"If he wants to kick your ass, he'll do it himself, at a time and place of his own choosing, but definitely not here. You're safe for the next hour."

Jonathan lifted his eyebrows. "Really. Well, that sure fills me with confidence."

Esme had been grateful that Jonathan had decided to play by the rules. She'd been conscious all day of not seeing him: not after the twins finally woke up and she gave them breakfast/lunch; not afterward, when she was with them in their giant sandbox, building a fort complete with moat (filled with water from the garden hose). Instead of coming to her, he'd left a cell phone message inviting her to a record-release party for a new ska band that he loved. Esme had called back to say yes, but that she wanted him to go with her to Echo Park first, to meet with Junior.

He'd been reluctant for so many reasons, not the least of which was that it struck him as some sort of macho game, two *cholos* battling over the same woman. From Jonathan's point of view—he'd told Esme as much—Esme was a grown-up. She could pick whom she wanted to be with; he and Junior simply had to respect her decision. Esme understood Jonathan's thinking, but once again it just reminded her that her boss's son came from another world, pretty much a foreign planet compared to her world.

They'd parked as close to La Verdad as they could. Esme was sure there would be no trouble, as the coffeehouse was kind of a flagship for the whole neighborhood; it was sacred ground.

"How long do we have to stay?" Jonathan wondered aloud. They edged around a rollicking family chattering away in Spanish. "I'd still like to get to that party."

"We'll see how it goes" was the best Esme could do. She'd tried to stay cool about this meeting, but as she approached the coffeehouse, she realized that her stomach was heavy with guilt. She should have gone to Junior herself and told him how it was. But no, she hadn't had the cojones to do it.

As usual, La Verdad was crowded and noisy, with people chowing down on Mexican pastries and drinking coffee and *horchata*. Some heads turned when Jonathan and Esme entered; there were whispers and titters. They all knew Junior.

"I'm doing this for you," Jonathan muttered.

"I told you, I'm sure it's fine," she assured him as he led her through the crowd.

Junior was sitting calmly at a rear table. He wasn't alone. A beautiful girl Esme recognized as Tia Gonzalez sat next to him, sipping a Coke. Tia was Esme's age, and had dropped out of school at thirteen when she got pregnant by a guy from Junior's old gang, Los Locos. This guy—Nardo—had been killed in a drive-by before his baby was even born. Tia's grandmother was raising the baby since Tia's mom was a junkie. This allowed Tia to do whatever it was that Tia did, which seemed invariably to involve changing her hair color every week or so. At the moment, her ebony hair was streaked with fiery red and crimped into long, frizzy strands that swung around her face; her eyes were heavily lined in kohl. She wore a red spandex T-shirt that was two sizes too small—exposing several inches of stomach— and low-cut enough that her breasts swelled above the neckline.

Tia saw Esme. Her reaction was to lean so close to Junior as to practically bury her pierced tongue in Junior's ear.

That could have been me, Esme thought, and not for the first time. To say Esme had no reaction to Tia's being all over Junior would be a lie. But her face betrayed none of her thoughts.

"Dejénos solos ahora, muchacha bonita," Junior told Tia, keeping his eyes on Esme.

He'd told Tia to leave them alone for a while, and he'd called her a pretty girl. Esme knew. Jonathan didn't. That didn't matter. The words had been said for Esme's benefit, not his. Tia rose and sauntered away on red velvet stiletto heels. Junior gestured to the two empty wooden chairs at his table. "Please," he told them.

Jonathan held out Esme's chair, then sat himself. The courtly gesture was not lost on Junior, Esme knew, but nothing at all showed on his face.

"Jonathan Goldhagen," Jonathan said, introducing himself. He put out his hand to Junior, who stared at it contemptuously.

"We don't need to pretend this is some happy occasion, gringo. You feelin' me?"

"The name is Jonathan. But yeah, I'm feelin' you."

"How's your shoulder, Junior?" Esme asked.

"I heal fast, *esa,*" he replied. "I got bandages under my shirt, but it's like I never got shot. So, okay, I didn't ask you two to come here to shoot the shit, we gonna get to it. You should have come to me 'bout this, Esme. But you didn't."

Esme flushed, because she knew he was right. What she wasn't sure about was how much Junior knew.

"I was in Jamaica with my employers," Esme explained.

"Yeah, and lover boy here wasn't on the trip," Junior retorted. "You think I don't got people watching your back, Esme? Watching *his* back?"

She should have known. To someone in Jonathan's world, Junior's devotion might have been a little scary. To Esme, it was strangely heartwarming.

"Okay, you're right," she agreed, not knowing where this was going. "Jonathan stayed here in L.A."

Junior leaned back against the wall behind him; the chair's front legs hovered in the air. "You miss him?"

Esme hesitated, her eyes boring into Junior's. Damn. What was she supposed to say? They were talking about Jonathan in the third person, but he was sitting two feet away.

"No," she finally uttered. "I needed some time to think. About both of you."

Junior's eyes grew narrow and he folded his arms behind his head. She noticed he didn't wince in pain. His gunshot wound really must have been healing. "Thinking time is up, *esa*. Time for action. Time to shit or get off the pot."

"Look, if I could just jump in here—" Jonathan began.

"Shut the fuck up," Junior snapped. His chair's legs slammed back onto the floor abruptly. "I'll let you know when you can speak. Esme?"

Esme could see that wasn't sitting well with Jonathan, so she put a restraining hand on his leg. No need to escalate things. Oh God, this was the moment she'd been dreading. She swallowed hard.

"Junior, I owe you an apology, eh? You're right. I should have come to you myself."

Junior barely nodded. He looked as if he was trying to

choose his next words very, very carefully. "So he's your man now? Is that it?"

Esme knew that in Junior's world, her world—*one* of her worlds—this was a yes-or-no question. It was shit-or-get-off-the-pot time. No middle ground.

"Yes," she said quietly, staring straight at him.

Junior nodded and tapped a large, blunt finger on the scarred table. He didn't speak for a long time. Then he directed what he said to Jonathan.

"Let me give you some advice, gringo. Every girl here in the Echo makes a mistake. That girl before? Tia, the one who was sitting with me? Her life is one big fucking mistake. I think Esme is making her big fucking mistake right now, but I know her a long time. She has to get it out of her system. I seen this shit before, with homegirls and gringos, *cholos* and white girls. They get dazzled. Then they get undazzled. No matter what happens, Esme is special, eh? You fuck with her, you fuck with me. You got that?"

"I got that," Jonathan agreed, his eyes blazing. "I care about her. A lot."

"I don't really give a shit how you *care*. I'm talkin' about how you treat her. Now get out of my face."

Jonathan looked bewildered. "That's it? We're done?"

Junior eyed him contemptuously. "Did I stutter?"

Esme reached across the table for Junior's hand, knowing it would be the last time she would touch it, touch him. She felt an ache behind her eyes, a catch in her throat. But Esme Castaneda never cried—not with all the things she'd seen in her life that would make a grown man weep—and she wasn't about to start now.

Her eyes met Junior's. There were no words to express how she felt. Better not to say anything.

She pushed out of her chair. Jonathan rose too.

"Esme?" Junior asked.

She turned to him. "Yes?"

"Usted es una estrella brilliante, ahora y por siempre."

She nodded, then followed Jonathan out of the coffeehouse.

When they hit the street, Jonathan exhaled loudly, as if he'd been holding his breath the whole time they were in there. "Well, that's what I call trial by fire. You good?"

"Yes." They headed for his Audi.

"So what did he say to you before you left?" Jonathan asked.

"It doesn't matter," Esme replied. Translating Junior's words felt like a betrayal somehow. And also, Esme was afraid that if she did translate, she really might cry. Because Junior had said: *You are a shining star. Now and forever.*

27

Lydia saw Billy as soon as he dashed into the Tower Bar at the Argyle Hotel on Sunset Boulevard; he was soaked from the driving rainstorm outside. Lydia was at the bar, drinking a virgin Mary—the idea of anything with alcohol in it turned her stomach. It was nearly eleven. The storm had come up out of nowhere, but it was just as well. Lydia thought it pretty well reflected how she was feeling on the inside.

Billy had called her that afternoon to offer another driving lesson that evening, but she'd explained that she had the kids until ten because Kat was coming back from the East Coast and Anya had decided to pick her up at LAX. So Billy had offered an alternative: he knew of this great bar, the Tower Bar, where an up-and-coming young singer-songwriter named Alexandra Munson would be at the grand piano. Lydia definitely needed to check her out. Lydia accepted the invitation gratefully—at the moment, being with Billy in a public place sounded wiser than a private place.

He smiled that darling, slightly crooked smile as he made his way across the room toward her, which looked more like a comfortable living room than a bar. Billy had said that the place had been featured on DailyCandy as being one of the great new places in the city to mingle and drink. With its wood paneling and upholstered chairs instead of barstools, Lydia did think it was beautiful. Off in the far corner, Alexandra was at the grand piano, wearing jeans tucked into slouchy boots and a black newsboy cap, wailing soulfully about lost love and betrayal.

Well, wasn't that just *perfect.*

"Hey," Billy greeted her, giving her a sweet kiss on the lips she had just slicked with gloss. "Man, it's a bitch out there, huh? There's like a dozen car accidents on the freeway. People have no clue how to drive in the rain." He nodded his chin toward her glass and slid onto the next chair. There was plenty of room; the rainstorm was keeping Los Angelenos home. "Whatcha drinking?"

"Virgin Mary," she replied.

He ordered a Guinness, then kissed her again, more slowly this time. "Much better greeting," he decided when he took his lips from hers. He nodded toward Alexandra at the piano. "She any good?"

"Just okay," Lydia lied. Truth was, the lyrics were hitting a little too close to home to be enjoyable.

"You lay with her and lied to me. . . ."

Lydia definitely did not want to listen to that. She turned to Billy, who slid a forefinger over her upper lip. "You look damn hot, did I mention that?"

Lydia was dubious. She'd thrown on a denim skirt she had hacked into a mini back in the rain forest and a white tee that she'd liberated from the lost-and-found at the country club—a treasure trove of clothing that was serving no useful purpose. "A million girls in this town are wearing some variation on this."

"Maybe," Billy allowed, "but it looks better on you. So listen, speed demon, when we doing driver's ed again?"

"This weekend?"

Billy nodded. "Works for me." The waiter slid his frothy Guinness onto the bar and Billy took a long pull once the foam had settled. "Oh hey, I've got good news. My boss is chattering about how he's getting his daughter a new Mustang, and he wants to sell her old Honda Accord."

Lydia frowned. "Wait, you mean Eduardo, the designer? I thought he was gay."

"Not exactly. He made that decision in the late nineties. Before that he lived near the WB lot in Burbank with his wife and three kids. He started cheating on his wife with guys, which is how he met his current lover." Billy shook his head in disgust. "Gay or straight, cheaters suck, huh?"

Lydia cocked her head to the side. "Well, some people are in relationships where they haven't pledged eternal troth, or whatever that's called. Maybe the two of them had some kind of an open agreement. For all you know, his wife was doing the gardener."

Billy shook his head firmly. "Nah, that never works. It's bullshit. You're either in a relationship or you're not."

Lydia gave him a noncommittal smile and took an uneasy sip of her drink. When she'd arrived at the bar, she hadn't decided whether or not to tell Billy about Luis. She figured that some boys would accept the news easily; especially because it would give them the freedom to do whatever and whomever they wanted to do. Others, though, might not, even if—like Billy—they had not yet extended visitation rights below the waistline.

Lydia wasn't sure what kind of relationship she wanted, but she did consider the previous night a mistake. Hell, yes. Once she'd gotten wasted, everything that had happened afterward was a big blur. That was not the way she'd envisioned losing her virginity. Now she wasn't a virgin and she *still* didn't know what sex was like. It really, really bit her butt.

"So you interested?" Billy was asking.

Lydia blinked. "Sorry?" She'd missed whatever it was he'd just said.

"I asked if you were interested in buying the Honda. It's really, really used, but it runs. He's only asking fifteen hundred dollars."

"I haven't got fifteen hundred *cents*, Billy."

"Wow, you really weren't listening. I told you I can loan you the money."

Well, things were just getting worse and worse by the minute. How was she going to explain that she now had a car, a car she had parked all day in a vacant lot down the street from the moms' mansion because she didn't want to face the questions from Anya? She couldn't. He'd ask where she got it. She'd say a friend. He'd say how close a friend, because "friends" don't go around giving "friends" cars. And she'd say . . .

Damn.

Billy didn't deserve games and subterfuge. He was so wonderful, in every way. Well, almost every way. If only he'd just come through in *that* way, she wouldn't be sitting there that very minute trying to decide whether or not to tell him about another guy who had come through in *that* way.

"Billy, there's something I need to tell you."

He sipped his beer, licking a little of the foam off his lips. So cute. "Yeah?"

"I . . . I . . ." She couldn't make herself say it. Just as she was about to, she thought of Billy and Becca, and their drunken tryst. She didn't want him to think that she was capable of *that,* even if his own experience might make him more likely to understand what had happened with her.

"You?" he prompted, setting his beer on the bar top with a heavy clunk.

"I . . . want to dance." She took his hand and tugged him away from the bar.

"There's no dance floor," he pointed out.

"Right by the piano is fine." She slipped an arm through the crook of his and led him over to where Alexandra was playing and singing, then wrapped her arms around his neck. He pulled her close and together they swayed to the sultry sounds of Alexandra's voice. This was where she wanted to be, and who she wanted to be with. She was sure of it.

There was still a lot to deal with, and one was a biggie. She hadn't gotten a morning-after pill, and didn't know where to go for such a thing. She didn't even know whom to ask.

Usually, Lydia was the girl with all the answers. As she danced in Billy's arms, for the first time she could remember, all she had was questions.

28

Kiley bustled around Platinum's guesthouse cracking ice trays into a large bowl and digging out the bags of junk food that had been there since before Platinum's arrest. Though it was late, Esme and Lydia were coming over. Kiley wanted to tell them about the incredible turn of events that had her back at Platinum's estate; her friends were happy to join her, even though it would be after midnight.

Her first day on the job had been very strange, because the colonel was a very, very strange man. When he said that Bruce had to have his lights out at twenty-two hundred hours—which translated to ten o'clock—and the little kids had to have lights out at twenty hundred hours—eight o'clock—he meant it. In fact, he proved it to Sid and Serenity by flipping the basement circuit breaker that supplied electricity to their rooms at exactly 7:59.99 p.m. (The precision had been achieved with his Marine chronograph, which featured timing to the hundredth of a second.) Bruce took the hint; his lights were out at ten.

There were two good things about the colonel. One was that he inspired confidence in other adults. When he and Susan had telephoned Jeanne McCann back in La Crosse, to inform her that Kiley was back at Platinum's property and that he, the colonel, was in charge and responsible for her well-being and safety, Jeanne had practically cheered. Kiley knew all this because the call had been made on the kitchen speakerphone. So there would be no difficulties on the parental front with this third job shift.

Second, the colonel was fair about Kiley's time. In fact, he'd informed her that once the kids were "down" (which reminded Kiley way too much of what they did to lame horses back in Wisconsin) for the night, her time and her guesthouse were her own. She was permitted guests up to a curfew of zero-two-hundred hours—2:00 a.m.

So she'd called Lydia and Esme, given them a brief recap on how it was that she was once again the nanny to Platinum's kids, and invited them over, giving them the evening's security code for the gate at the bottom of the hill so that they wouldn't have to awaken anyone at Platinum's mansion. Lydia had babbled something about not needing a ride, she now had a car. Kiley had found that peculiar, since she wasn't aware that her friend had a driver's license. Esme arrived first, in faded Levi's ripped at the knees and a vintage Santana T-shirt. Her hair was tied back in a long braid; she wore no makeup. Kiley got her a Coke, and before Esme could say much about her conversation with Junior and Jonathan at La Verdad, Lydia was at the door.

She arrived in a new burnt orange cashmere sweater trimmed in what Kiley thought was sable.

"Not hardly. No animals were harmed in the making of this ensemble." Lydia laughed. She explained that the sweater had been sent to Anya as an early birthday present from relatives in St. Petersburg. A girl who could skin a monkey knew a lot about fur; Lydia could tell it was a very high-quality fake. But she convinced Anya that her relatives had, in fact, sent her real Russian sable, knowing that the moms were extremely antifur. Lydia suggested that rather than fire off an indignant letter to her well-meaning relatives, Anya simply donate the sweater to Goodwill. And now, Lydia explained blithely, her friends could just call her Good Will.

It was just so typically Lydia.

Kiley brought the packages of Doritos and chips into the living room, put them on the coffee table, and curled up on the couch, legs tucked underneath her. She wanted to hear about Esme's trip to Jamaica. She'd heard that the ocean there was so crystalline that you could see fish swim thirty feet away.

But the ocean wasn't what Esme talked about. Instead, she told them about the Silverstein brats, the delicious prawns and ackee on the beach, and losing the twins at a sugarcane-cutting festival.

"This girl Tarshea, she saved my ass," Esme concluded. "Seriously, if it wasn't for her, I wouldn't even have a job anymore. She wants to come to America. I think we should try to help her get a nanny job."

"Oh, really?" Lydia asked, perking right up. "I hear Evelyn Bowers is looking."

"We can't place her with someone crazy," Esme warned.

"Well, that lets out everyone in this town," Kiley cracked.

"Okay, here's what we'll do," Lydia began, tapping a thoughtful finger against her chin. "I'll stand in the breezeway at the club with a tall glass of iced tea, and when someone comes to poach me, I'll explain that I'm merely a proxy."

"Let me offer a more practical idea," Esme said dryly. "I'll keep bugging Steven and Diane. They'll finally say if you want her to come so much, find her a job yourself. Then we get hold of Tarshea and have her send information about herself, pictures and child-care references. Then go to the breezeway."

Lydia nodded. "Now see, we make a hellified team."

A half hour later, Kiley had Esme and Lydia almost crying with laughter, regaling them with stories about her adventures in nannydom and her return to the land of Platinum. Lydia was most interested in the Paulsons' home-gym orgy. All Kiley would say was that she'd never be able to look at Animal Planet in quite the same way.

"Speaking of Animal Planet . . ." Lydia padded across the heavy carpet atop the hardwood floors and flopped onto one of the two beanbag chairs by the small fireplace. She let the rest of her sentence hang in the air.

Kiley got the gist immediately. "You and Billy?"

"Um . . . no," Lydia admitted.

Esme and Kiley exchanged looks. "Someone else?" Esme ventured.

"Remember Luis from the country club?" Lydia asked.

Esme's brows knit together. "The golf pro from Costa Rica who was flirting with you? That guy?"

"That guy." Speaking matter-of-factly, Lydia recounted the story of her driving lesson, the drinks, the dancing, the champagne, the car, skinny-dipping . . . and everything else.

For a long moment, they were all silent.

"So . . . is that what you wanted?" Kiley finally asked.

"At the time," Lydia admitted. "But I was drunk, so . . ."

Esme made a face. "Drunken sex with a guy you don't know. So sophomore year."

"I didn't go to high school," Lydia pointed out. "Besides, I'm not the first, and I won't be the last. I'm not counting it."

Esme raised an eyebrow. "Because?"

"Because I don't remember it. The first time I really, really have sex, I will definitely remember."

"Did you remember to use birth control?" Esme shot back.

"Umm . . . not me."

"Him?"

"Don't know."

Esme shook her head. "Grow up, Lydia. Tomorrow, Planned Parenthood. Morning-after pill and STD tests. I'm taking you. No arguments."

"Joy," Lydia pronounced, but nodded gratefully.

Kiley chewed a sliver of ice from the bottom of her glass of Coke. "You saw Billy tonight. That must have been fun. What did you tell him?"

"Nothing." Lydia pushed the choppy bangs from her forehead.

"Nothing?" Kiley echoed.

"Y'all, I was going to," Lydia insisted. "But then . . . it started to seem like a real bad idea."

"I thought you were Miss 'I Blurt Everything,' I don't care what people think."

Lydia gave her a cool look. "I'm becoming Americanized."

"Meaning you're learning how to lie," Esme surmised.

Lydia sat up, looking ruffled. "Girlfriend, what about you and Junior and Jonathan? People who live in mud huts shouldn't fire blow darts. Or however that saying goes."

Esme stood up and stretched her arms over her head. "You're right. I'm not really on your case, Lydia. I'm on mine." As quickly as she could, she filled her friends in on the three-way meeting at La Verdad that evening with Junior and Jonathan.

"But it's what you wanted," Kiley reminded her.

"Yes, it is," Esme agreed. "But . . ." She caught her lower lip with her teeth. "Sometimes I think I don't know what I want. The look on Junior's face . . . it nearly killed me."

"That is exactly why I have turned over a new leaf," Lydia maintained. "Dishonesty is the best policy." When Kiley and Esme laughed, Lydia came back over to the couches and nudged Kiley with her foot. "Your turn. Did you and Tom finally do it?"

"No," Kiley admitted. She stood up and paced the room, trying to find the right words. "I like Tom so much."

"So does the entire female half of the free world," Lydia quipped. "Plus all the gay men in West Hollywood, according to X. Come to think of it, I'd bet those Calvin Klein billboards have tempted many a straight man too."

Kiley stopped by the doorframe leading to the kitchen, leaned against it, and sighed. "Well, maybe that's the problem. Maybe I'm just not—not confident enough to deal with that." She told them about the gorgeous model they'd run into at Cafe Med, and how Tom had introduced her to the model as his "friend Kiley."

Lydia waved a dismissive hand. "That's what has you upset?

Guys hate to say 'girlfriend.' Then, after they get married, they hate to wear a wedding ring. Anthropologists have found that those two phenomena cross cultural boundaries."

"It was in a magazine," Kiley and Esme intoned at almost the same time.

"Now, see, y'all just assume that I don't know anything first-hand," Lydia chided them. "I remember my mom telling me a long time ago that my father was one of the few married men she knew who actually wanted to wear a wedding band. And when the Amas are what we'd call engaged, the girl and the guy pierce their lips with matching sticks." Her voice dropped con-spiratorily. "Many a young Ama guy does not keep that stick in place when his lady friend isn't around, I'm here to tell you."

"Well, maybe I don't want to be with the kind of guy who can't say 'girlfriend' about me," Kiley said.

"Tell you what," Lydia began brightly, "I think we've proved that I'm not nearly so picky about commitment. How about I have sex with Tom and then let you know if it's worth your while?"

Kiley laughed so hard her stomach hurt. Even Esme looked less tense than she had when she'd arrived. Kiley thought for the zillionth time what a huge difference having two close friends made in her life. She didn't know how she would have gotten through the insanity of the past few weeks if it hadn't been for—

Back in the bedroom, her cell phone rang. She wondered who it could be. Not the colonel—he would have used the hotline between the main house and the guesthouse that Plat-inum had installed. Lydia and Esme were here with her. It was too late in Wisconsin for it to be her mom. That meant it was ei-ther her best friend from home, Nina, or Tom.

"Excuse me," she told her friends.

Nina she could deal with. Tom, she wasn't quite sure what she'd say, or how she would say it. Maybe she was just way too Wisconsin to deal with a supermodel. But God, he was so hot. And nice and sweet and . . . "Hello?"

"Kiley? Hi, it's Jorge."

Jorge. Esme's friend, whom she'd stayed with after the arrest. It took Kiley a moment to process this, so sure had she been that Tom or Nina would be on the other end of the phone call.

"Jorge! Hi."

A beat of silence.

"I know it's late. If this is a bad time—"

"No, no, it's fine." She sat on the edge of her bed's flowered quilt. "How are you?"

"Fine. I thought I'd see how your new nanny job is going."

Kiley nearly laughed out loud. Which nanny job was he talking about? Evelyn? The Paulsons? "Actually, I'm back at Platinum's," she told him, explaining the situation.

"That's great. Better for the kids, that's for sure. Your mom must be happy."

"She is." Kiley bit at a hangnail. She was going to tell him that Esme and Lydia were here with her and that she had to go, but something in his voice led her to think that he'd called for a specific reason.

"So listen," Jorge continued. "Tomorrow night the Latin Kings are performing at the Hideaway—it's a club in Panorama City, out in the Valley. Another group canceled at the last minute and we got called to fill in. It'll be our first gig outside of the Echo."

"Good for you. You must be excited."

"And nervous," he admitted. "Anyway, I thought maybe you'd like to come. You never did get to hear us perform at La Verdad. It would be nice to see a friendly face."

Why, why, why were boys so vague? What did this invitation mean? Was he inviting a lot of people, or was this more personal? How could she find out without sounding like an idiot?

"Would you like me to pass the word around?" she asked. "Like to Esme, Billy, Tom . . . the friends I was with at La Verdad that night?"

"Not really."

Kiley waited for more, but Jorge was silent. Maddening. She needed clarity, dammit.

"Okay, Jorge, this may sound incredibly dumb and I apologize and . . ."

Just say it, Kiley.

"Are you inviting me as . . . a friend?"

"For starters," he said. "After that . . . maybe more. In other words, I am asking you out."

Clarity. At long last, actual clarity. That was so great. That was so—

Jorge had just asked her out. What should she do? Should she say no because she already had a boyfriend? Should she rush into the living room and clear it with Esme? After all, he and Esme were best friends, and she'd suspected that Jorge had a serious crush on Esme. Should she tell Jorge she'd call him back, then phone Tom and wake him up to say, "Yo, you have competition now, so just what the hell do we mean to each other? Please put it in writing and have it notarized."

No. That would be stupid. Maybe she was asking too much of Tom, too soon. Maybe it was just his overwhelming good looks and attractiveness to other girls—men—everyone!—that made her want clear parameters from him.

Then, in that moment on the phone with Jorge, it was as if the clouds parted and she finally saw something important about herself. She had a bad habit: she wanted guys to define relationships for her, when the truth was that she needed to define them for herself. As much as she liked Tom, as much as she was attracted to him, if he wasn't ready for her, she definitely wasn't ready to be tied down to him.

"Kiley, are you still there?" Jorge's voice pulled her out of her musings.

She answered, firmly and clearly: "Yes. And I would love to go out with you."

About the Author

Raised in Bel Air, Melody Mayer is the oldest daughter of a fourth-generation Hollywood family and has outlasted countless nannies.

Tainted Love
a nannies novel

coming May 2007